SHERLOCK HOLMES AND THE HOUDINI BIRTHRIGHT

Here, two areas of mystery are linked: the exploits of Sherlock Holmes and the secrets of master escapologist, Harry Houdini. Doctor Watson's collaborator, Sir Arthur Conan Doyle, finds himself drawn into the world of the fake psychics and Houdini is anxious for Holmes to unmask the perpetrators who prey on the innocent believers. Once he has been torn away from his bee-keeping activities, Holmes's investigations lead him to some surprising locations, including a Ruritanian castle.

VAL ANDREWS

Sherlock Holmes and the Houdini Birthright

Complete and Unabridged

LINFORD
Leicester

First published in Great Britain by
Breese Books Limited
London

First Linford Edition
published 1998
by arrangement with
Breese Books Limited
London

British Library CIP Data

Andrews, Val
    Sherlock Holmes and the
    Houdini birthright.—Large print ed.—
    Linford mystery library
    1. Holmes, Sherlock (Fictitious character)—Fiction
    2. Watson, Doctor (Fictitious character)—Fiction
    3. Dectective and mystery stories
    4. Large type books
    I. Title
    823.9'14 [F]

    ISBN 0–7089–5292–5

Published by
F. A. Thorpe (Publishing) Ltd.
Anstey, Leicestershire

Set by Words & Graphics Ltd.
Anstey, Leicestershire
Printed and bound in Great Britain by
T. J. International Ltd., Padstow, Cornwall

This book is printed on acid-free paper

Part One

The Sleuth, the Scribe and the Sorcerer

THE events which I am about to relate started in the summer of 1922 at a time when I was in part-time medical practice in North London. My friend Mr Sherlock Holmes continued the while to philosophize and tend his apiary on the Sussex coast. I had never ceased to marvel at the seeming ease with which he had made the change from consulting detective to country gentleman. During the first several years of his retirement I had a half expectation that he would return eventually to his old haunts and that the game would be afoot as of yore. But, as with bereavement, time had been the great healer and the winter nights when I dozed before the fire to dream of a sharp shake of my shoulder and an even sharper admonishment in that incisive Sherlockian tone became fewer and fewer.

Of course Holmes and I kept in touch, spending an occasional weekend together either at his Fowlhaven retreat or, when he came to London, at the Railway Hotel at Charing Cross. A meal at Simpsons, a recital at the Albert Hall and he would be off again upon an early morning south-bound train. However, there were one or two episodes which were of sufficient note to hold his interest and make him cast his retirement aside for a while as if removing a comfortable cloak, only to replace it as soon as a task was completed. In other words, a taste of that which had been his food and drink was not enough to make him return to the table.

He had been good enough, at my request, to assist my old headmaster, Doctor Locke of Greyfriars, to resolve a problem. Then later, towards the end of the Great War, he had been persuaded by Lestrade of Scotland

Yard to investigate a bizarre case involving the violent death of a Chinese mandarin, shot dead in front of two thousand astonished people. There had been other examples of occasions when Holmes had returned to show that he had lost none of his old cunning.

However I am allowing myself to become sidetracked and must return to the matter in hand. I should mention at this point that I have never quite managed to make my peace with that modern irritation the telephone. This instrument produces not only an alarmingly shrill ring but the most strange and eerie of disembodied voices.

The voice in question held the added complication of a strong American accent. "Am I speaking to Doctor Watson?" Assured that this was so the voice continued, "Harry Houdini speaking, I want to contact your old partner Sherlock Holmes. I tried that address on Baker Street but he seems to be out of town!"

"My dear Mr Houdini", I replied, "I remember you well but Holmes has been out of town, as you put it, for the better part of twenty years, for he retired to Sussex to keep bees in 1903." This information produced a gasp, followed by a short silence, then the voice of Houdini continued strongly, "Boy am I behind the times! I can't imagine Sherlock rusticating on a bee ranch. Say Doc, is he still a smart cookie, I mean . . . does the old guy still have all his marbles?" After I had assured him that Holmes was still in possession of all his faculties he went on, "Well I'm over fifty myself now, but I'm not quite over the hill either as you may have heard." I had, for one could scarcely lift a newspaper other than *The Times* without seeing the name Houdini in bold headlines. I had recently learned for example that he was to become a star in the moving pictures.

Seemingly reassured that Holmes was as shrewd as ever, Houdini continued,

"I have just got to see him Doc; it's really important to me and I've come all the way from the big country, mainly just to consult the only guy in the world who can help me. I haven't forgotten that last time when he saved my hide, all those years ago. So can you tell me where to find this joint in . . . Sussex did you say?"

"Mr Houdini, Holmes trusts me to guard his privacy," I replied, "I would have to assure myself that your business would be important or intriguing enough for his retirement to be interrupted."

His tone became quieter and milder as he said, "Then let me call and see you Doc, then I can show you something that might make you want Holmes to get involved." What could I do save give him my address and a time when I could see him?

The figure that entered my study later that same day was familiar enough in that his obviously expensive clothes looked rather as if he had slept in them. Twenty years had broadened him, thinned and greyed his hair and somehow contrived to make him appear to be of even shorter stature than ever. His handshake was hearty as he said, "Doc, it's real good of you to see me for I know that you must be busy with your sick people and of course with your writing. I notice that you are still documenting the exploits of your buddy Sherlock."

"You manage to obtain *The Strand* in America?"

"Oh sure, we get it all the time. Bess reads it and she tells me all about the latest Holmes's adventures."

I muttered something to the effect that the editor of that journal still demanded more and more Holmes's exploits as his reader's demands were insatiable. "It has become more difficult since his retirement as I can only present old cases which had somehow managed to slip through the net in the past. Of course Sir Arthur Conan Doyle prepares the final drafts from my notes and diaries."

Houdini's broad brows knitted. "Sir Arthur is a good friend of mine, which is part of my problem." He sat pitched forward in a straight-backed chair and refused the glass of sherry which I offered him (Holmes of course would have remembered his total abstinence).

"Surely such a charming and accomplished gentleman could scarcely present you with a problem?"

"The guy is a doll and Lady Doyle is a gracious lady and I wouldn't want to offend either of them for anything. You'll remember that Sir Arthur and Mr Holmes were the two people who helped me the most when I first hit this country around 1900. In trying to crash the big time I was a carnival worker out of my depth. Sir Arthur used his influence with Scotland Yard to set up my first big gaol escape and Holmes helped me to effect it. After my success here I never looked back and the Doyles have been my friends ever since. In fact we only disagree on one subject."

"And that is . . . ?"

"He is a great believer in spiritualism, which as a religion I can respect. But I could never make Sir Arthur understand that there are sharks in the water. Most people are gullible and inclined to place their faith and trust in those who would deceive them for financial gain. But Doctor Watson, I'm a magician, so I have been in the deception business from way, way back. Say I know that business from A to Z. It takes one to know one. I know deception when I see it and I tell you I have seen it at every seance that I have attended where the medium stood to gain from it. Now with Sir Arthur being involved with you guys in the logical explanation of the mysterious and seemingly unexplainable you might expect him to be as sceptical at least as the next man. But no, for during my campaign in recent years against psychic frauds he has been my most severe critic."

To tell the truth, whilst I was not entirely uninterested, I was beginning to wonder where Houdini's narrative was leading and where the necessity came for the involvement of Sherlock Holmes. I glanced at my watch and he sensed concealed impatience.

"OK. Doc, I know time is money better than anyone so I'll get straight down to cases. When I lost my own dear mother about ten years ago I was all but desperate with grief. I spent the next several years in making a sincere investigation into the possibility of making spiritual contact with lost loved ones. I attended over a hundred seances before I decided that this was not possible. The mediums fell into two main categories. There were those who were hucksters who tried to deceive me in return for money. Of course I could see through all their deceptions and exposed them. The rest were honest and sincere people who looked for no

11

financial gain but produced no results. As I have said, I exposed many of the frauds but not before they had the chance to convince Sir Arthur of their genuine psychic spiritualistic powers."

All of this I found interesting and I did indeed find it surprising that friend Doyle had proved to be so gullible. Of course, even if Houdini was right in his accusations of fraud, one had to bear in mind that Sir Arthur and Lady Doyle had lost a much loved son in that dreadful conflict of 1914. I could still not quite see why Doyle's convictions should trouble the dynamic little American so much. In fact I said as much, even if not in those very words. Houdini's response was surprisingly erudite for that of a self-educated man.

"The fact that Sir Arthur's beliefs differ so much from my own would be merely a minor bone of contention between us were it not for a couple of recent episodes. The first of these concerns a highly respected doctor and his wife, Doctor Robert Blackthorne and Mrs Marina Blackthorne. The lady claims to be a very powerful medium. Doyle managed to get me in on a seance she held. I've seen a lot of frauds as I've told you Doc, but this dame was the best ever! Many of the things she did I could easily figure, others I am still working on. But the Doyles have swallowed it all, hook, line and sinker. If the Great Houdini can't explain it all to Sir Arthur what chance to convince him that this Marina is a charlatan?"

"Can you be sure that she is just that, for you tell me that you cannot explain all that she does?"

"She is a fake with a capital F!"

"Is it not possible that she is capable of both genuine psychic contact and deception used merely as a form of insurance?"

"You mean a shut-eye? No, she's a fake, I feel it, I know it but I can't prove it."

For the first time since Houdini

had entered the room there was an uncomfortably long silence. I knew not what else to say and he seemed reluctant to continue for such a loquacious man.

At last he said, "The other matter is even more embarrassing but I'll put my cards on the table Doc. A few weeks back Sir Arthur and Lady Doyle were in the States where Sir Arthur undertook a lecture-tour. As you can imagine the man who discovered Sherlock Holmes is a big draw, back home." (I found this a little irksome because I had myself discovered Sherlock Holmes, as he put it. Sir Arthur had merely transformed my scribblings into readable episodes for the masses.) "But his subject this time was to plead the cause of spiritualism. After the tour the Doyles went to Atlantic City to rest and they put up at the Ambassador's Hotel, inviting Bess and me to join them. In fact we took a room adjoining theirs and the four of us spent a lot of enjoyable time together, mainly on the beach, strolling the boardwalk and taking in the sights. One day Sir Arthur tells me that his wife has become greatly interested in automatic writing."

I was not familiar with this particular form of graphology and asked him to explain more fully. "Well Doc, the medium holds a pencil loosely over a sheet of paper. The spirit or guide, or whatever force is supposed to be at work, takes over and actual readable messages get written. Well, sir, he invited me to their room, just me without Bess, for a demonstration. I couldn't very well refuse and Bess was tired so it worked out quite well. In any case I was interested to see what it was all about."

I too was anxious to know what it was all about and begged him to continue, which he did. "He closed the drapes and Lady Doyle sat there at a table upon which were pencils and paper. Sir Arthur bowed his head in prayer, which he insisted I join them in and held his wife's hand as if trying to activate her in some way. I was told to close my eyes, not opening them again until I heard a tapping noise. I then saw that Lady Doyle was tapping the blunt end of the pencil on the table. Now don't get me wrong Doc, she was not trying to do it secretly to fool me into thinking they were spirit raps. No, she was doing it quite openly as if it was part of some sort of ritual. She claimed that some great force was making her do it. From then on there did seem to be some intimation that the pencil was moving other than from her own wish. She glanced upward and asked if there was anyone there. She tapped the pencil — or it tapped, three times — and she told us that this meant 'yes'. She asked if my dear mother was there and said a lot about how long I had waited for some sort of message or sign. Then quite suddenly she upended the pencil and, placing the point on the sheet of hotel notepaper, she made a cross with it or, as she put it, the pencil did. After that I tell you,

16

Doc, I was all but scared by the ferocity with which she started to write on the paper and all the time her eyes were tight shut. She went on like this for three or four minutes and then stopped suddenly, seemingly exhausted. When she had recovered a little she asked Sir Arthur to open the drapes and she handed me the paper. It was covered with small, neat handwriting conveying a loving series of messages for me. Lady Doyle said that it had all been written by a Cecelia Weiss, which was my mother's married name. The phrases, which were easy enough to read, were all to the effect that she was happy and making a home for me in paradise for when it was my time to join her. She went on to say how happy and grateful she was to have finally made contact with me after trying so hard for so long. I tell you, Doctor Watson, I was far from dry-eyed by the time I had finished reading. I so much wanted — want still — to believe."

He tailed off and I thought for a moment that he was going to weep. Compassion took a hold of me and my heart ruled my head as I asked unwisely, "Then, why man, why not believe and be happy?"

He pulled himself sharply together and said, "Doctor one either believes or one does not. All my past experience tells me that this is not a genuine spirit message. If I believed in it I could not continue with my campaigns and spookbusting shows if I had even a passing doubt. But you know the Doyles, how could they be other than absolutely sincere? They are not the sort of people that I have been gunning for these past ten years! I, Houdini, debunker of those who claim to be able to communicate with the dead, cannot, dare not allow myself the doubts which this has all but produced in me."

He threw upon the table before me a neatly folded sheet of light blue notepaper. I unfolded it and there it was just as he had described it. Headed with the crest of the Ambassador's Hotel, Atlantic City, the paper was covered with the small neat handwriting of Lady Conan Doyle.

I tried to read more into Houdini's problem than was there in his plea. There he was, the stocky tub-thumping little showman from America, a fascinating character, a monopolist of the world's headlines for more than twenty years. Was he sincere in his dilemma or did he perhaps want to use the name of my friend Sherlock Holmes to gain even more publicity? Yet I felt that his problems presented some interest that might intrigue Holmes, who might perhaps never forgive me if I did not at least give him the chance to decide for himself whether he wished to become involved or not.

Eventually I said, "Mr Houdini, I feel that what you have told me is of sufficient importance to at least bring to the attention of my friend. Only he can tell you if he will become involved. Like myself he is of course a man of science but with a mind open enough to consider your problems from every aspect. Whatever his firm beliefs he discounts nothing."

I wired Holmes that Houdini and I would visit him at Fowlhaven upon the following afternoon (he had still refused point blank to install a telephone). When I suggested to Houdini that we catch a certain train upon the morrow from Victoria he would have none of it. Despite all my mild protestations we eventually journeyed to Fowlhaven in Houdini's hired Mercedes, complete with uniformed chauffeur.

The pleasant parlour of Holmes's rural retreat was aged yet functional enough to have withstood, seemingly without protest, twenty years of misuse. Spilled chemicals seemed to have done less damage than had been the case at Baker Street. As we entered the room I noticed at once Holmes collapsed in a wing chair. He was wearing a black alpaca jacket, strong tweed trousers and linen of perfect presentation. His feet were encased in carpet slippers but I was happy to see that their Turkish cousin still hung upon the wall, well filled with dark shag. His appearance was immaculate if casual and the lines around his eyes were of concentration rather than age. The still dark widow's peak of his hairline was just about holding its own. Although lean, he was, it appeared, in good condition for a man of some seventy years. He worked hard on a calabash, producing clouds of acrid blue smoke.

With the windows closed despite the season, breathing difficulties were caused for both Houdini and the elderly Scots lady who had admitted and announced us. (She was one of a series of housekeepers who came and went; all forced to answer to the name of Hudson.) He rose and with only a hint of arthritis shook me warmly by the hand. "My dear Watson, how good it is to see you, it has been months. Mr Houdini, the years have broadened you and I notice that you have become somewhat short sighted."

Houdini grinned, "Do I squint that much?"

"Not at all but the marks upon your left cheek and below the eyebrow indicate the fairly frequent use of a monocle. Not the kind with the gallery; rather a glass disc with a milled edge."

Houdini dangled such an optical aid upon the end of a silk cord. "I find it more handy than specs, which I can never lay my hands on when I want them. A sign of age I guess."

"Oh but still spry enough to do a little dancing, at least at an afternoon function at, I think, the Ritz Hotel."

It was the turn of the man who had amazed millions to be astounded. "Say I don't remember telling either of you that I was staying at the Ritz or that I had been onto the dance floor!"

The old detective smiled enigmatically, "The Great Houdini does not reveal his methods. But alas I am just a retired detective who must explain how it is done lest his deductions be disregarded as pointless or sheer guesswork. By the way I note that you are absent-minded and sartorially careless."

"That's me! But say, how do you know all this stuff?" Holmes threw me the ghost of a wink and said, "You are wearing patent leather boots, normally reserved for formal affairs. This tells me that you are not only forgetful but careless about your appearance; the traces of blue chalk on the boots indicating a recent excursion onto a dance floor, probably that at the Ritz where that particular blue chalk is employed. The fact that you are absent-minded, well, you have already told me that yourself in explaining that you have difficulty in remembering where you have left your spectacles."

The magician was delighted, "Bess and I were at the Ritz and I got pulled out onto the dance floor, though not to dance, rather to perform a few parlour tricks for the guests."

"Ah you see Watson, I am losing

my touch. I should have realized that a celebrity might venture onto a dance floor other than to waltz or do the polka!"

"But you are still astonishing Mr Holmes, enough for me to beg for your aid." Then Harry Houdini told Holmes everything that he had told me, from the death of his mother, through the campaign against fake mediums and he climaxed his narrative with the story of the automatic writing. He tossed the folded sheet of hotel notepaper onto the table with a gesture that held the desperation of a gambler playing his final card.

Holmes, who had listened with rising interest, studied the writings carefully, enlisting the aid of a lens. He waved it at Houdini saying, "More reliable than a monocle and far more powerful!" He returned to the study of the writings. Eventually he said, "Mr Houdini, spirits may or may not exist, I can doubt but cannot discount their existence. Let us assume that there are spirits and that of your mother is anxious to contact you. Why do you suppose she would need to do this through a third party?"

I dared to interject, "Perhaps an expert is required rather like an interpreter?"

Holmes snapped at me, "You assume that our loved ones, having passed on, communicate in a language other than their own. This brings me to a point concerning this so called spirit writing. What was your mother's name, for I assume that Houdini is a *nom de théâtre*?"

Houdini replied, "Of course, my real name is Erich Weiss and my mother was Cecelia Weiss, but her maiden name was Steiner. She was a very small lady and my father was a rabbi. In 1874 they emigrated to the United States from Hungary to escape ignorance, persecution and anti-semitism but they never really settled down in America . . . "

Holmes interrupted with a question,

"You were yourself born in the United States?"

I fancied that Houdini was slightly uncomfortable with the question but replied to it quickly enough, "Why, er yes, soon after they arrived, in Appleton, Wisconsin."

I could see that Holmes had noted the slight hesitation, though he did not press the point, instead saying, "Please continue with your narrative."

"My father was unable to obtain employment as he spoke no English and my mother never learned more than a few words. But to me she was like a queen. In fact after I first made it big I was able to buy for her a dress made for Queen Victoria, which Her Majesty had never worn. I took her on a trip back to the old country and put on a ball for her in Budapest. All our kinsmen and others who had called us losers and no-hopers came and mother was a queen for a night in Victoria's gown." He stopped, realizing that he had been all but carried away with

26

his oratory. Indeed there had been a shake in his voice. He recovered quickly having given us a very small demonstration of that quality which had made him a very great showman.

Seemingly unmoved by the histrionics, Holmes said, "Quite so, Cecelia Weiss, née Steiner, a Jewish lady who spoke no more than a few words of English. Did she speak German, Hungarian, Yiddish perhaps?"

Houdini nodded, "German and Yiddish fluently and she spoke a little Hungarian."

Holmes pointed to the cross at the top of the paper and said, "In view of all this information I find it hard to believe that your mother, a Jewish lady who spoke and wrote practically no English should write these messages so faultlessly, more in the style of a titled lady than that of a simple emigrant. Moreover, would she be likely, spirit or no, to mark the head of the paper with the sign of the cross?"

"Wow, how could I have missed

something like that? The perfect English should have told me and the sign of the cross! But don't get me wrong Mr Holmes, Lady Doyle is a dear sweet woman and I just know that she must have believed what she was producing to be genuine spirit writing."

Holmes agreed and I added, "The human mind, especially that of the devout believer, can play some incredible tricks."

The king of escapes and magic, far from being jubilant as might have been expected from one who had gained the point as he wished, was obviously still in a dilemma which he expressed in words. "What must I do Mr Holmes, surely you can see my problem? I have vowed to expose all spook frauds as I call them but the Doyles are sincere. There is the problem of this doctor and his wife Marina."

Houdini had not given Holmes as much detail about Doctor and Marina Blackthorne as he had earlier presented to me. So he rectified this omission with a detailed account of the seance which he and the Doyles had attended. Holmes asked if he had explained the fake methods, which he had spotted, to Sir Arthur.

Houdini replied, "Sir Arthur quite failed to see why Marina should have used trickery just because it was possible for her to have done things that way. Moreover, there were these phenomena she produced which I could not explain. Sooner, if not later, the papers will get hold of the fact that I have seen that which I cannot challenge. My career, in recent years, Mr Holmes has been very largely based on the fact that I am a spook-buster. I have even offered large sums of money to any medium who can produce the unexplainable under test conditions. Marina will, I feel sure, gain enough confidence to attempt to ruin me before long."

Holmes was thoughtful for a while and we had to wait until he had recharged his pipe before we heard his voice again. Then, through clouds of blue smoke, he thrust his great bill of a nose in Houdini's direction, "I would have to sit in on one of these seances myself in order to be of any real help. Do you think you could arrange for this to happen?"

The magician shook his head sadly, saying, "I doubt if the Blackthornes would put on an act for Sherlock Holmes."

"But perhaps they would stage a seance for the Reverend Septimus Carstairs? Clerical impersonation has always been one of my specialities and such roles have proved more than helpful in past investigations, as Watson will tell you. I will put up at the Charing Cross Railway Hotel under that name and in that disguise. There are rooms there that can be hired to hold a seance."

This planned deception and the fact that Holmes had clearly agreed to become involved in Houdini's problems cheered the American noticeably. He proved to be a hearty trencherman when Holmes insisted that we all sit down to a repast of cold cuts which he and I washed down with tankards of the local cider. Houdini took only fresh water with his meal, in between the extraction of silver coins from bread rolls and a number of other extremely amusing and puzzling parlour tricks.

Afterwards, over coffee, Holmes said, "I have no miracles to show you in return Mr Houdini, except to say that although I have never met your brother I can appreciate that the two of you are very much alike, at least at a glance and from a fair distance."

Houdini started, "And you say you have never met Theodore, or Dash as I always call him. Perhaps you have seen his picture somewhere?"

Holmes denied this, "No, but I have read this morning's newspapers. Most of them carried an item to the effect that only a few hours ago you had been thrown, manacled and encased in a heavily weighted packing case, into the Hudson River."

"Tell me Mr Holmes, did I escape safely?"

"Evidently so! Even the Great Houdini cannot be in two continents at the same time. Obviously then you were impersonated and, knowing that you had a brother in the same line of business as yourself, the thought became obvious. Indeed he must be very like you indeed to pull off such a deception. Not one of my major deductions!"

Houdini laughed again, "But to be serious, you make it sound so easy. Yes, I had to be in this country of yours to sign some contracts and arrange for promotion of *The Man from Beyond* when it is shown in London. That's a motion picture by the way. I had arranged the Hudson River stunt months ago and could not cancel it. So Dash and I figured out how to get me out of trouble; not as difficult as all that because we had done the same thing and got away with it way back.

He's taller than I am but, if he parts his hair like mine and keeps well back from the people, there is no problem. But just because you have made light of your deductions, as you call them, this does not mean that I am going to tell you how I knew that you had selected the three of spades!" We all laughed as he referred to a card trick that he had shown us minutes earlier.

I did not return to London with Houdini, preferring to accept an invitation from Holmes to stay the night and return upon the morrow. Houdini departed in the late afternoon, leaving it with me to arrange the details that we had all discussed. As the big Mercedes purred its way towards the London road I re-entered Holmes's parlour to find him taking a bulging file from the shelf which held his scrapbooks. He said, "No question of looking for H in the books Watson, Houdini has so much written and published about himself that he requires a dossier of his own."

I was amazed. Not only with the fact that Holmes had this bulging folder on Houdini but that he continued to keep up with all this research material at all.

He read my mind when he said, "Oh yes Watson, the habits of a lifetime do not change with rustication. I will keep up the books and files to my dying day. I will leave my collection to Scotland Yard."

As we sat and sorted through the piles of newscuttings Holmes asked me, "What do you make of friend Houdini and his problems Watson? Am I wise to involve myself in them?"

"I believe that you are doing so more for the sake of Sir Arthur than for him."

"Well, it is true, that like yourself, I have a great respect for Doyle but I have long noted the ease with which he can be manipulated. Do you recall, for example, the case of the two schoolgirls who convinced him that they had captured the images of fairies at the bottom of a garden with a Box Brownie camera? He was far from pleased with me when I proved to him beyond doubt that the whole thing was a hoax."

"He so desperately wanted to believe in fairies, Holmes. Maybe at heart we all did. When you showed him the fairy figures cut from a story book and arranged among the grass and stones you all but severed a connection that has been invaluable to us all. It has, after all, made Doyle a fortune, provided me with a livelihood and turned you into a legend in your own lifetime."

"You flatter me Watson. Why there are even those who believe me to be a figment of Sir Arthur's imagination. One scholar has expressed in print that Sherlock Holmes was really Sir Arthur's tutor, Doctor Joseph Bell. I have rather mixed emotions concerning my notoriety. I probably would not have retired from active practice at such an early age had Sir Arthur stuck to his historical novels. I became altogether too well known with the public at large to follow my profession comfortably."

I was a little taken aback by his words. Of course Holmes had always seemed a little uncharitable in his comments upon his adventures as presented in *The Strand*, but it had never occurred to me that these published exploits could have been worse than a minor irritant to him.

"Had I realized the extent of your disapproval I would have long ago ceased to make the material available. Really Holmes, you should have said something to me upon the subject."

"And ruin a profitable sideline for a good friend who would otherwise have been just a struggling doctor? Oh no my dear Watson, I could not have been so cruel!"

I was embarrassed and, as soon as I decently could, I switched the conversation from Sir Arthur Conan Doyle to Harry Houdini. "What do you make of Houdini?" I asked him.

"Oh much the same as I made of him twenty years ago Watson," he replied. "A self-made man who has pulled himself up by his boot straps. Despite his fame and fortune he is a man of spartan habits. The expensive clothes and the Mercedes are of no real interest to him, he simply feels that the trappings of wealth are expected. He has a friendly and open manner but, surprising in a professional deceiver, he finds it difficult to disguise his emotions. Did you notice for example the very slight hesitance of manner that he displayed when I enquired as to his place of birth? When, after some seconds of hesitation, he told us Appleton, Wisconsin, he all but blushed. Why, I wonder?"

I too had noted these things but made less of them than did my friend. "Could it be that Appleton is the kind of small town which would seem unfashionable for a great showman to claim as a birthplace?"

Holmes shook his head, "I think not, he claimed Jewish immigrant parentage with pride. The man is certainly no kind of a snob. No matter, it seems of little importance."

But I noticed afterwards that Holmes had pencilled question marks beside all the printed references to Houdini's birthplace that occurred in the cuttings from the file.

* * *

A few days later found Holmes — or rather the Reverend Septimus Carstairs — comfortably installed at the hotel at Charing Cross. I put up at that same establishment for the convenience of being on hand should Holmes require my help. After so many years it was wonderful to be sharing an adventure with him again even if it was as yet but to abet his impersonation of a reverend gentleman.

The first day was spent in establishing Holmes's new identity; just to make sure that it was deceptive enough for his purpose, that of convincing the Blackthornes that they would be putting on a demonstration not just for the already convinced Sir Arthur, but also for a simple cleric.

Meanwhile, Houdini had not been idle having contacted his friends the Doyles and the Blackthornes to arrange a seance. He took luncheon with us at the hotel — where we occupied a secluded corner of the dining area — and put us into the picture concerning these arrangements.

"I have talked with Sir Arthur and Lady Doyle and I'm pleased to tell you that their attitude is fine, great in fact," he said. "They actually *want* another seance with the Blackthornes and are more than happy to let the Reverend Carstairs in on it as an impartial observer." Then he turned to me, with just a touch of embarrassment and said, "No offence Doc, but I guess you will need to get lost when the time is near. The Doyles know you pretty well and with due respect you are not an actor, or a master of disguise like Mr Holmes here."

"No false whiskers for you Watson," Sherlock agreed, "but I feel sure that, as ever, your co-operation will prove invaluable if you stay in the background." I accepted the situation with reasonable grace and was glad to hear that Houdini had not encountered any difficulty in hiring a suitable room in the hotel for the seance.

Houdini pushed his plate aside. "Well gentlemen, it's all fixed for eight tomorrow night. Meanwhile if you would like to spend an hour or two studying the sort of people that you are going to be up against I suggest that you attend the demonstration of spirit contact being given this afternoon at the Blandford Hall. My face is too well known, but do go to see and hear for yourselves, I tell you you'll get a kick out of it!"

At about two-thirty we left the hotel and sauntered as far as Oxford Street by way of the Charing Cross Road. Thence we took a motorized taxicab and reached the Blandford Hall only a few minutes after the appointed time for the demonstration.

In the lobby we encountered a dark-haired woman of indeterminable age who asked us to sign the book as she handed us our tickets.

"Admission is free is it not?" I enquired having assumed this from a glance at the poster tacked to the noticeboard outside the building.

She nodded, saying, with a voice and air of resignation, "You are allowed, of course, to make a donation towards the hire of the hall and other expenses. This is, of course, not a profit-making enterprise." Rather sheepishly we slipped a few half-crowns into a box on the table which appeared to be quite well filled already.

Professor Bernard was already upon the platform and addressing the audience when we entered the auditorium. He was a doleful-looking man of about five-and-thirty, dressed in black. He was neat though hardly immaculate although his luxuriant dark hair and Dundreary whiskers were obviously well tended. He spoke with a voice which sounded as if it had been made rock-hard through many years of projection.

"They are all around me at this very moment ladies and gentlemen, all jostling each other to gain my attention. What's that? Yes, I'll tell her if you think that she is here . . . you do?" He spoke and gesticulated towards what I could be forgiven for considering to be an imaginary presence. Certainly not one which was visible.

"Is there a lady with the initials M S present?" There was no response, so he continued, "Oh M F, I do wish you would slow down and speak more distinctly."

He was interrupted by an elderly lady who sprang to her feet and fairly shouted in excitement, "My initials are M F . . . Mary Fraser!"

The professor smiled at her benevolently, "Mary . . . of course I knew you had to be here . . . your friend is here, Jane . . . or is it Janet . . . or Jean?"

Again he seemed to be having some difficulties with the enunciation of the disembodied voice which he alone could hear.

"No, it *is* Jane, Jane Bradley!" the lady responded, "Oh please tell me what my dear friend wishes me to know?"

"She seems anxious about another friend, one that you both knew during her earthly life." As this statement elicited no response from Mary Bradley, the professor continued, "I'm sorry, she will speak so rapidly, slow down you silly girl . . . what? It's about your dear little friend, your companion . . . it's . . . "

Mary Fraser started, "It's Jock, my little dog. He was off-colour when I left home, please ask Jane if he will soon be well again?"

The response was reassuring, "Mary,

Jane says do not worry about your dear little friend, he will be well again soon if you stop giving him chocolates and lumps of sugar. Jane has to leave now but Mary wants to contact you again soon through me. Please remain seated at the end of my demonstration and we will talk about this."

The old lady nodded happily as she sat down, her face wreathed in a most attractive smile. The professor turned his attention to another spirit. One after another, he reunited a Mr Godfrey Sheridon with his cousin George and a Miss Smith with her fiancé who had lost his life in the Great War. A fallen soldier wants — with the initial J — wants to contact his dear sweetheart."

A lady of some thirty years leapt to her feet crying, "John, is it my dear John at last?"

The professor listened to the voice which only he could hear and then asked, "Was he in the Royal Engineers?" This drew an instant "Yes, oh yes, dear

John it is really you!"

The demonstration continued much in this manner for an hour and was then interrupted by the lady we had seen at the ticket table who shyly stepped onto the platform holding a small sheet of what looked like personal notepaper. She handed it to the professor who glanced at it and dismissed her with a wave of his hand. After he had studied the paper, he said, "The lady who has written this note must realize that I cannot reply to such a personal matter in public but if she would like to remain seated after the demonstration I will be happy to consult her and try to help."

After that the professor's demonstration went from strength to strength as he reeled off the full names of departed ones with superb histrionics. Then suddenly he asked, "Is there a Mr Watson here, a Mr J Watson?"

I replied, "My name is Watson, Doctor John Watson." I confess to being somewhat startled as he went on to say, "Quite so, but our dear departed do not use the titles of formality. Your brother is with me and wishes you to know that he is now quite without those demons which had possessed him in life."

It appeared to me at the time that the message could only come from my late brother who had died a drunkard.

Holmes nudged me and said, "Come Watson we have heard enough old chap. Let us leave and partake of tea at the Polytechnic". His manner was kindly but firm.

It was but a short walk to the tea house and we were soon installed at a table with teapot, cups, milk jug and the extra hot water upon which Holmes always insisted. We had spoken little on the short walk from the hall, my own thoughts being centred upon the seeming message from my late brother and Holmes's silence being obviously out of consideration for me. He poured the tea and then broke the silence. "Well Watson, did you ever see such an example of a rogue feeding off the sorrows of the bereaved before?"

"I admit some of it did smack of chicanery," I said, "for example, the vagueness concerning the names of both the bereaved and departed. It was as if he waited to be prompted by the people in the audience who wished to believe; blinding themselves to obvious trickery. As an actor he rivals the late lamented Sir Henry Irving!"

"Obviously the professor has his methods as I do myself but Watson you speak as if you had reservations concerning his psychic powers."

"Well, I could see how he *could* have deceived those poor souls but how did he know that I had a brother who died a hopeless drunkard? After all there would hardly be another Doctor J Watson in the hall in a similar situation."

It was quite uncanny to hear the sage words and incisive voice of Sherlock Holmes issuing from the lips of a benevolent cleric as he said, "My dear

Watson, let us consider the whole thing. To begin with he simply announced a name, J Watson, which you had yourself signed in that book when we entered the hall. You told him yourself that you were John Watson, *Doctor* John Watson!"

I considered what he had said but found a flaw. "Even so, how could he be aware that even a J Watson would be present. He had already started his demonstration when we entered, he did not leave the platform and had no opportunity to look at that book."

"Oh Watson, what of the fictitious letter from a lady in the audience brought onto the platform by his confederate?"

"You mean that letter was really just a list of some of the names that had been written in the book?"

"Exactly! Had we stayed longer I have no doubt that even more well-defined names would have emerged."

I had to confess that I could well have been taken in by crafty subterfuge until another point seemed to nag at my logic. "But Holmes, you know very well that my brother died a drunkard. You of all people should recollect it for did you not once all but terrify me when you used your methods of deduction in an examination of his watch?"

Holmes nodded seeming as kindly as his disguise itself. "My dear fellow, it is you yourself who have applied this particular interpretation. The professor's exact words did not imply a connection with drink."

"He said that my lost one was now without those demons that had possessed him — words to that effect."

"Quite so, no mention of drink, the demons could have meant pain or a troubled mind or freedom from debt or any of the things so often coincidental with bereavement. I would remind you that he did not even mention that it was your brother that he referred to. To coin a phrase, old fellow, you wrote your own scene."

Of course he was right and the more I thought about it, the more obvious it all became, illustrating the ease with which the bereaved and innocent-minded are deceived. But to what purpose, for the admission had been free, with the coins in the collecting box possibly being sufficient to pay for the hire of the hall, but more likely not.

As usual Holmes managed to read my thoughts, saying, "Although there seemed no obvious profit motive I am sure that the professor, as he calls himself (although professor of what I would like to know) probably gains a handsome living from giving private consultations with the spirits, involving those people whom he bade to remain seated at the conclusion. I have even known such charlatans to become beneficiaries from the wills of their elderly victims."

I changed the subject but only fractionally. "So, Holmes, do you think that Houdini sent us to that demonstration in order to alert us to the kind of thing we might expect from the Blackthornes?"

"I think he considered it might be an excellent curtain raiser. He wanted our minds to be directed into a certain way of thinking. If the Blackthornes are *not* genuine I think we must expect deceptions to make those that we have just experienced seem elementary Watson."

He had opened the discussion even further. "You think then that we might find Mrs Blackthorne, or Marina, to be a genuine medium or psychic, or whatever she claims to be?"

"As a man of science and logic I have always considered any kind of supernatural occurrence to be unlikely. You will notice the word that I use, I say *unlikely*, but not impossible. Even if a thousand such people were proved to be fraudulent the thousand-and-first could still be genuine. We must not discount anything Watson."

★ ★ ★

On the following day I had to consider my plans carefully. I knew that I would need to absent myself from the hotel well in advance of the arrival of the seance participants. I consulted Holmes about this at breakfast, or rather he brought it up by saying, "Watson what are your plans for today? The Doyles and the Blackthornes may arrive early so I suggest that you absent yourself by late afternoon. I can give you an account of the seance if we meet for coffee in the hotel lounge at about 11 pm."

"You think they will have left by that time?" I asked.

"If they do not show some sign of departure by ten I will feign exhaustion to speed it. To make quite sure, however, I will tell the lobby porter, Grimes, to watch for your return and appraise you of the situation. He can be relied upon as I have discovered that he was one of our 'irregulars' at Baker Street some thirty years ago."

So it was that I left the hotel at about

four and made my way to the British Museum where I spent a pleasant hour in the Egyptian gallery. I felt some slight guilt at thus spending my time in self-indulgent pleasure but I had been assured by Holmes that there was little that I could do to aid him until after the seance. I mused that there might be little enough that I could do even then, so I tried to put the whole matter out of my mind for a few hours.

Having taken tea at Fullers, I took a stroll down to Fleet Street where I dined and eventually made my way to the Embankment thinking to take a brisk walk there in the direction of Charing Cross. I had not been walking long beside the wide-topped parapet when I espied a young woman, neatly and respectably dressed, sitting upon one of the public benches. Her attitude was one of complete despair; her head was in her hands and her shoulders shook as if from sobbing, although I heard no sound. There were few other people about and as I drew nearer she rose quite suddenly and, with a scream, made for the parapet with great speed. Something in the despair and urgency of her movement plus that scream told me that she intended to throw herself into the Thames.

Immediately I spurred myself into action without quite realizing the form that it would take. I managed to grasp both her arms as she tried to clamber up onto the stone wall. She struggled a little at first but then, quite suddenly, her resistance ceased and I was able to calm her enough to enable me to guide her back to the bench.

At first I scarcely knew what to say to her but eventually I seem to remember saying quite a lot. "My dear young lady I thank providence that I happened by at this exact time to prevent you from taking a step of the kind from which there is no retraction. After all, every cloud has a silver lining and it's another day tomorrow, don't you know?"

She had calmed a little and I was able to appreciate that, despite her expression of anguish, she was extremely attractive. She turned upon me the most amazing and enormous blue eyes and said, in educated tones, "Sir, nothing that happens tomorrow can alter my situation. I came to London just two days ago to join my fiancé. I arrived a day earlier than expected and, upon arrival at the hotel where I knew him to be staying, I was horrified to discover that far from being alone he was with a young woman who was improperly dressed. He had tried to conceal her in a wardrobe but all the signs of a liaison were there and eventually, knowing that I was not deceived, she emerged."

I sympathized with her as best I could, "What a blackguard! I trust you will have no more to do with him!"

"Indeed not, sir, but my situation is now impossible. You see there was a violent quarrel with my parents who did not wish me to marry George — Major Armitage that is."

"An officer but no gentleman."

"Quite, sir, but I was deceived by him so completely and have burned all my bridges. I have no resources and am untrained for any sort of trade or profession."

"Of course not but surely suicide is not the answer?"

"Sir, for a woman alone in a big city, hungry and penniless there is no other answer except . . . "

I protested at once, "Good heavens, you must not even consider *that* hair!" To my relief she said, "Of course not, I would prefer death but just as I had worked up the necessary courage, you came along."

I tried to be constructive, "Come I feel sure that there is another answer." I took a notebook from my pocket and scribbled an address upon a leaf which I tore off and handed to her. "Here is the address of an organization which exists to aid distressed gentlewomen. If you present yourself there tomorrow morning I feel sure that they will house you in their hostel and arrange for you to obtain employment as companion to a lady or something of that kind. What is your name dear lady?"

"Kate Courtney-Smythe'.

"Well, Miss Courtney-Smythe, I will write a short recommendation on the back of one of my cards. I feel sure they will take heed of it."

I wrote a short and apt message on the back of my visiting card, signed it and handed it to her together with the scrap of notepaper.

She took them both eagerly, studied them and then said, "Oh sir, Doctor Watson, what a splendid plan. You have saved my life and I will always remember you with gratitude. You were right, every cloud perhaps does have a silver lining and it can only be providence that sent you to prevent me from doing such a terrible thing. God bless you!" She embraced me, with gratitude rather than passion, "It will not be quite so bad sleeping here on the Embankment in the knowledge that it is only for one more night."

I was horrified, "You have been sleeping rough?"

"I have had no option. When I left my parents I had little more than enough for a single train ticket. What was left I spent upon an inexpensive meal; but that was on Thursday."

"You have not eaten since?"

"No, but I feel more optimistic now."

"You have luggage?"

It appeared that she had placed her bags in the left luggage office at Victoria. I knew that there was only one thing to be done. "Look here, we can't have you in this situation any longer. Here is a five pound note which will enable you to reclaim your luggage, have a meal and put up for the night at the ladies-only hotel at the back of Victoria Station."

At first she shook her head and pushed the proffered bank note aside, "No sir, you have done so much for me already, I cannot take your charity."

"Nonsense, it is not charity for you

have my card. Although I will be staying at Charing Cross for a day or two I should be back at my home address in about a week. When you are on your feet again you can repay me."

Tears welled up in her great blue eyes as she took the bank note in a small, trembling, gloved hand, "Doctor Watson as I know that you are a gentleman I will accept the money as a loan. God bless you again sir and now I will go and reclaim my luggage, get a meal and find that hotel." I was about to offer to accompany her but, kissing her hand to me, she suddenly crossed the road and was very suddenly lost to my view. I was sorry to lose her company so quickly but consoled myself that I would see her again when she called to return my bank note. Perhaps, I mused, she might even consent to dine with me.

Then as I sat and pondered upon the good fortune that had allowed me to prevent a dreadful tragedy these thoughts were disturbed by the arrival of a police constable.

"Excuse me, sir, but did I see you giving money to a young woman?"

I answered curtly, "Why yes, but I fail to see how it can concern you!"

"That depends on what you was a given of it to 'er for, sir!"

For a moment or two his words seemed to make no sense. Then suddenly his meaning dawned upon me. I snapped, "Really, constable, you are impertinent in the extreme. Do I look like *that* sort of person?" I handed him one of my cards then added, "I'll have you know that I am a doctor and a colleague of Sherlock Holmes. If you must know I was assisting a distressed gentlewoman, a Miss Courtney-Smythe, stranded and destitute through no fault of her own."

The policeman laughed and said in a most impudent tone, "Oh, so she's on that game now is she? I know young Kate, we've 'ad 'er inside for soliciting often enough but I didn't know she'd taken up the suicide lark!"

I was furious. "She seemed a most respectable young lady who but for my intervention would have taken her own life."

"Not 'er sir, quite a few of the girls 'ave given up their reg'lar game in favour of this suicide one. They wait for a likely type, such as yourself, to come along then pretend to be just about to throw themselves into the river. The mug prevents them, gets a sob story and ends up givin' 'em money. Wonderful actresses some of these girls, reg'lar Sarah Bernhardts some of 'em!" He saluted me, then walked off at a regulation two-and-a-half miles an hour.

I sat there for ages ashamed that I had been so easily duped, pondering upon how much of the story to tell Holmes. But eventually I decided to tell him none of it on account of his having enough upon his mind. As I walked to the crossing that would take me back to the hotel I saw another woman similarly dressed but this time ignored her.

★ ★ ★

I entered the Charing Cross Hotel at exactly eleven of the clock and was relieved to be approached by the lobby porter who with a broad grin said, "Doctor, Mr Holmes and the American gent would be glad if you would take coffee with them in the lounge." This meant that the coast was clear with the Doyles and the Blackthornes evidently no longer on the scene. I nodded my thanks and walked to the end of the lounge where I could see the angular cleric and the much smaller but stocky figure of the magician.

At this late hour we had no fear of being within earshot of eavesdroppers, not that we expected any such presence.

"Watson, do join us," said Holmes, "I see you have been in dalliance with a lady with dark hair and about five feet three inches tall." I grunted, my plan to keep from him the affair on the Embankment thwarted. "Hair on my lapel Holmes?"

"No, Watson, traces of face powder."

I went through the motions of expressing the obvious. "How does face powder tell you her hair colour?"

"Because women, Watson, powder their faces with powders that are graded in shade to match or rather complement their hair. I have made quite a study of it, because it has its uses in identifying crime suspects. There is a monograph on my shelf at Fowlhaven."

I swiftly changed the subject. "How did the seance go?"

"For me Doc," replied Houdini, "it was like the good old curate's egg, good in parts. By which I mean that I could easily see through some of their deceptions and, indeed, there were deceptions. But I confess myself baffled by couple of things that they pulled off. Sir Arthur and Lady Doyle were most impressed and he is more convinced than ever about the existence of spirits and the ability of some to communicate with them. But I'll let Mr Holmes tell you about it."

Tell me about it Holmes did, in very great detail: "They are a plausible couple Watson, these Blackthornes. He is a doctor and has great sincerity of manner. She is an attractive lady in her thirties with rather startling auburn hair. They allowed Mr Houdini, Sir Arthur and myself to examine the seance room thoroughly and, of course, we could find nothing unusual as they had not themselves had access to it. It contained simple furnishings only, as they had requested. A few chairs, a small four-legged table and a gramophone with one or two records of discreet orchestral music. Then Doctor Blackthorne, who proved to be a small, neatly and soberly dressed man, took from an attaché case a few simple objects which he said they would use just to concentrate the attention of the spirits when they were unable to speak. These consisted of a small bell, rather like that which rests on the table before us now — used to summon a waiter — a slate, some chalk and a phosphorous-treated trumpet, rather like a small megaphone.

"Lady Doyle was taken to an anteroom where she was allowed to watch Mrs Blackthorne as she changed from her dress into a kimono. We were assured that it was obvious that Marina — as Mrs Blackthorne liked to be called — was not concealing anything untoward about her person. Meanwhile, we checked the doctor's pockets in a similar way. Then we gathered in the seance room and Marina took a seat at the table, facing the door. She placed the bell on the floor under the table and the slate with a piece of chalk lying on it flat on the table near where she sat. The trumpet she placed at the opposite end. We had examined all these objects once but were invited to do so again, which we did. Then Sir Arthur was invited to sit on Marina's left and Mr Houdini on her right. Each held one of her hands and they were each instructed to place a foot lightly upon one of hers. This meant that she could move neither hand nor foot without their being aware of it, or so she explained. She said that under normal conditions in a seance for believers this would be unnecessary. These precautions were entirely for Houdini's benefit so that he would not suspect any sort of trickery.

"The doctor and I sat near the door so that he could operate the light switch. He insisted that his right hand be left free for this purpose which seemed a reasonable request, but I held onto his left hand. In other words free hand or no, he could not move from his chair or go within a yard of the table without his movements being detected.

"Lady Doyle sat in the remaining chair on one side of the table. The curtains were extremely thick, so once the light was extinguished the darkness was as complete as possible.

"Before being seated the doctor had

66

started the gramophone that the music might put both medium and the spirits into a suitably calm mood. He sat down and extended his right hand, extinguishing the single overhead light.

"To the strains of *Lieberstraum* Marina explained, 'We are here in order to help the spirits of the dear departed to try to make contact with those here with us. We will try to contact the dear mother of our brother, Harry Houdini and the beloved son of our dear friend Sir Arthur Conan Doyle. We may or may not succeed and other spirits may be attracted, some of these may even be of a malevolent nature. But no harm can come to anyone save possibly myself. Please do not switch on the light, Robert, unless I request it.'

"Then she explained that she would go into a trance and started to hum and sing softly to herself, occasionally stopping to enquire 'Is there anyone there?'

"After about half-an-hour a voice was heard, quite unlike Marina's and like that of a roughly spoken artisan. There followed some conversation between Marina and Wallace (which she explained was the name of her guide in the other world). Wallace sang bawdy songs and used coarse language which I would not have expected Marina or Lady Doyle to approve of or even understand. Wallace explained that he had a message for 'the old lady and gent' doubtless referring to Sir Arthur and Lady Conan Doyle.

"He explained that their son had not been on the other side long enough to speak to them as yet but would make a sign of his presence by causing the trumpet to move. This it did, most noticeably due to the luminosity that it had. In fact the trumpet all but floated in circles and swayed around before once more settling in its original position. At this point I should explain that every time the gramophone records finished playing, Robert Blackthorne released my grip and felt his way round to switch it off and replace the record before starting it again. But always he did this quickly and I retained my grip on him at all times when his aid might have seemed to be helpful to Marina.

"She requested the light to be turned on only once, when Houdini's mother had been contacted and, she claimed, had written a message for him on the slate. A word was seen upon the slate, the word LOVE. Several times there were voices of various kinds including that which was claimed to be that of General Gordon, still complaining that the reinforcements had not arrived in time to save him at Khartoum and a child who piped that he had been a sweep's boy, 'Lorst hup the chimberley in 1860!' In fact it was a most professional and convincing demonstration but the *piéce de résistance* was yet to come.

"Sir Arthur and Houdini were requested to place their free hands lightly palms down upon the table. Lady Doyle, who had both hands free, was requested to do the same.

There was then a terrific groaning and moaning from Wallace and evidently, I was afterwards assured, the table started to rock and raise itself up in a truly eerie manner.

"Remember not only were both Marina's hands encapsulated but both of her feet were restrained by touch. Finally, after the table had ceased to rock and roll the little bell under the table started to ring. When it ceased, Marina called, 'Robert, please, the light!'

"Her voice was shaky and none too distinct and when the light was switched on she could be seen to have slumped onto the table.

"After she had been revived by Robert and Sir Arthur who chafed her wrists and sent for glasses of brandy, she spoke quite strongly again, 'There was a mischief-making spirit which got quite out of control.'

"In speaking to the Blackthornes afterwards, Mr Houdini assumed his usual air of disbelief but the Doyles were full of praise, completely convinced that their son was trying to make contact and would eventually be able to speak at a future seance.

"It was my turn to speak and this simple cleric expressed delight with the seance. I then told them that I was myself something of a medium, 'though only a tyro in comparison with yourself dear lady' and promised that I would attempt to give them a slight demonstration if they would care to return the following night.

"They agreed to this and, by the way Watson, I asked if Sir Arthur's colleague, Doctor John Watson, might be permitted to attend also, feeling that your light has been hidden under a bushel in this matter long enough. They expressed no suspicion or objection and Doyle was delighted with the idea."

I should explain to the reader that during Holmes's narrative Houdini had made the odd interjection, reminding Holmes of various points, his comments always showing the sharpness of his mind.

Now it was Houdini who spoke to me at some length.

"That's a pretty good picture of what happened Doc and, of course, Mr Holmes and I have discussed it all since the others left. Your friend should have been a magician because his mind works like mine. We were agreed in the essential details of most of the deceptions that were involved. We figured that Doctor Blackthorne operated a small pair of lazy tongs with which he was able to lift and gyrate the trumpet."

"Where did he get them?" I asked, "surely you would have spotted them however cursory your search of his clothing?"

"They were in the gramophone Watson," replied Holmes, "he picked them up after the search, in the act of placing the needle on the record."

"Right and he got rid of them again the same way in switching it off, or rather changing the record," Houdini added. "That way he was prepared for any sudden suggestion that he should be searched again."

"How about the word chalked onto the slate, that could surely not have been managed the same way and in the dark?" I asked.

"I imagine she picked up the chalk with her mouth," explained Houdini. "It was fitted into a small metal holder so that she could have manoeuvred it between her teeth and used it that way. Not easy in the dark but she has undoubtedly done it many times before. She's had a lot of practice at writing by mouth."

"Were there any signs of chalk around her mouth when the lights went on?"

Holmes chuckled, "She would have had the sense to lick her lips before that happened, right Mr Houdini?"

The American nodded, continuing, "The bell she rang with her foot, grasping it with her toes."

I remonstrated, "Come, surely both her feet were held down by yours and Sir Arthur's?"

It was Holmes who continued, "We are agreed that she withdrew one foot from a shoe. Possibly she even had an aperture cut from the foot of her stocking allowing the toes to be more easily moved. This would not have been noticed when her shoes were on."

"Would the shoes perhaps be hard-topped, so that they would not collapse under your own feet when her foot was withdrawn?"

"Exactly and I fancy that there were needle-point spikes on her sole and heel so that the shoe would hold steady on the rug even without her foot being within," Holmes replied.

Houdini was impressed, "Wow! That's a refinement that I had missed." He took a notebook from his pocket and scribbled in it, delighted at this small detail, saying, "One more little point for my spook-busting demonstration!"

As far as I could see, Houdini and Holmes between them had explained the methods by which the Doyles had been deceived — except for one manifestation which they had not mentioned. "All very well, but what about the floating and rocking table?"

Houdini's brows knitted, "Doctor Watson, I admit myself baffled, which is not good. Unless I can explain everything that Marina does, I can't go to the Doyles and hope to get them to believe that they have been duped."

"Oh I think I can help you there Mr Houdini," Holmes said, smiling. "It puzzled me at first, but I think I have the answer. I have considered all possibilities commensurate with the conditions involved and have decided that the least likely answer is the right one. The method is I believe of the simplest possible nature, therefore simple of execution and undetectable afterwards. Holmes enjoyed having us both on the edges of our seats. He took a Turkish cigarette from a case and lit it with a vesta. (He had decided that a pipe was unsuitable for this particular impersonation yet could not exist for long without strong tobacco.) After what seemed like an age he said, "She lifted and moved the table with her head."

Houdini started, "Her head . . . you mean she ducked it down beneath the table and lifted it?" Holmes nodded, hardly needing to say more.

Houdini threw back his head and laughed, "Of course, it's perfect! Mind you, it would be difficult to be absolutely sure that she did it that way but I agree that it's likely. In any case another perfect item for my spook show."

Holmes suggested that we should examine the seance room before the hotel staff had a chance to clean it. This we did with great thoroughness. The first thing that Holmes looked at carefully was the carpet beneath the table, which I was assured was still in the position it had occupied during the seance. He dropped on his knees, peering with his pocket lens. He chuckled and said, "There are small holes, like those produced by needle points, just as I expected. So we were right about her ringing the bell with her foot." He turned his head upward in order to talk to us and his gaze lit upon the underside of the table. There was a whoop of joy unbefitting an elderly clergyman as he jumped to his feet and spun the light table to show us its underside. "See! There are, providentially, some splinters just under the edge which have trapped some extremely distinctive reddish hairs!"

Sure enough it was just as he said. There they were, long hairs of that particularly unusual auburn tone, which must surely have exactly matched Marina's.

"Well Mr Holmes you are a marvel!" Houdini was delighted. "I don't figure there is any other way or reason for those hairs to be there, it's obviously just as you deduced. Now why don't we take a look at that phonograph?"

We did then, indeed, examine the gramophone and Holmes pointed out some telltale scratches on the edges of the sound chamber. "You see, these marks have been recently made by a sharp metal edge. What a pity we did not examine it before the seance. Mind you, I am a detective and not a clairvoyant."

It was a gratified Houdini who left to join his wife at the Ritz, vowing to meet us at seven on the following evening.

After he had gone Holmes and I took a nightcap in the lounge which we were able to enjoy without Houdini's disapproving gaze. When we had exhausted the present possibilities of the matter in hand, Holmes pressed me a little further on my dalliance with the lady on the Embankment. I told him the story in full, finishing it by saying, "So you see, even after all these years of experience through association with yourself, of the criminal classes, I was easily deceived."

To my amazement Holmes was far from remonstrative. "Come Watson, just because the policeman told you of this particular ploy it does not follow that you were its victim. You told me yourself that you saw another young woman later on. Was she dressed in anything like the style of this lady with whom you spoke?"

"Why yes, they both wore grey and had green gloves."

"There you are, it may be that the second lady was the confidence trickster referred to, whilst the young lady you gave the money to could conceivably have been genuine. You are a good judge of character, Watson." He cheered me up a little and I said, "Alas, we shall never know."

"On the contrary, if she was genuine she will return your money."

I couldn't help feeling that taking on the garb of a priest had softened Holmes somewhat.

* * *

On the following morning Holmes knocked upon my bedroom door at an unreasonably early hour. I remonstrated. "Holmes, it is not yet eight, breakfast is not served for nearly an hour. What is making you disturb me so early after we have burned the midnight oil?"

"Good old Watson, as ever unchanged in a changing world! Had I not stirred you I'm sure you would have slept until ten. But we have work to do and your share of it will involve an errand which cannot be too long postponed."

We were the first to be seated at the breakfast table and Holmes did not even have the decency to allow me to finish my bacon and eggs before explaining his plans.

"Watson I have an errand which will take me to Leicester Square, the purpose of the errand will be revealed to you in due course but I want you to go to Fleet Street to see my friend Richard Hawke at the *Daily Falcon* office. I will give you a note explaining a favour which I need from him. Naturally I will take you into my confidence and explain to you that which I require leans heavily upon a long acquaintance. I will rely on you to press and explain the urgency of the matter."

He passed the note to me which I read quickly with, I confess, a growing amazement. "Holmes, do you really think the matter is important enough to ask Mr Hawke to take such pains?"

He looked at me as severely as his benevolent disguise would allow. "Watson, *you* considered it important enough to summon me from the peace of the Sussex coast and become involved in it." I could think of no answer.

Alas, dear reader, I cannot, at this point, reveal the exact nature of either

81

Holmes's errand or mine. These things will be explained in their proper order lest you might feel like one reading the first and then final page of what is now known as a detective story (a genre quite unknown by that term when Sir Arthur first developed my diaries before the century's turn).

Shadows were growing longer by the time Holmes and I conferred again in the hotel lounge. We compared notes upon our separate expeditions and discovered that all had gone as planned for us both.

Holmes said, "This may well be the final occasion on which I will be forced to wear this wretched cassock and dog collar. I will be glad to get back to my bees and my books, yes, and above all, my pipes!" He stubbed out one of his seemingly endless supply of Turkish cigarettes.

"Surely it is permitted for a clergyman to smoke a pipe?"

"Have you seen the style of pipe that is in character for a man of the cloth? Most effete and incapable of holding more than a thimbleful of the most stringy and mild tobacco. These Abdullas are at least satisfying without arousing any sort of incongruous appearance. If I am not mistaken I think I can see friend Hawke in the near distance."

Sure enough the journalist was soon seated beside us, having first placed a copy of the early evening edition of the *Daily Falcon* upon the tea table.

"Mr Hawke, please allow me to pour you a refreshing cup of tea?"

The man from Fleet Street blinked at Holmes, "I don't think we have met before, padré, yet you know me by name. Watson here asked me to meet him and Sherlock Holmes."

My friend lowered his voice so that he could speak in his normal tones, "Come Hawke, I am glad that my disguise is good enough to deceive a sharp-eyed newspaper man!" He glanced at the newspaper upon the table as he poured tea. Hawke soon accepted Holmes's disguise without further show of surprise. He had been on the spot for many of Sherlock's dramatic exploits and more than a couple of aliases.

"As you will see, I did manage to get our printers to run off a single copy of our early evening edition with an altered front-page headline. As you suggested in your letter, I got them to make it the secondary front-page story. I agree that this is more convincing. The death of Sherlock Holmes would make our front page but not our banner headline."

Holmes nodded and having glanced at the paper he passed it to me. I read it with a sort of dreary fascination. There was a twenty-year-old portrait of Holmes, under the announcement BAKER STREET DETECTIVE DIES! There followed a story (as I am assured they call it in Fleet Street), the first paragraph giving details of Holmes's demise from a heart attack at his home on the Sussex coast where he had resided since his retirement in 1903. His age was given as sixty-nine (which was as near correct as I am able to ascertain). There followed several other paragraphs detailing Holmes's life and career, including highlights of some of his most famous cases and exploits. The article finished, "Mr Holmes had few close friends but doubtless his passing will be greatly mourned by his close colleague Doctor J H Watson, and Sir Arthur Conan Doyle, who collaborated to bring some of Holmes's greatest triumphs and adventures to the attention of the readers of *The Strand* magazine."

Although of course I knew the whole thing to be contrivance — for was not my friend seated beside me — yet the small hairs on the nape of my neck still crept at its realism. I was reminded of that dreadful day so many years earlier when I had been led to believe that Holmes had plunged to his death in mortal combat with his arch enemy.

"It is depressingly convincing Mr

Hawke," I commented.

The newsman smiled, then nodded. "Then perhaps in return, gentlemen, you would explain to me what it is?"

Between us Holmes and I explained everything about Houdini, the Blackthornes and the involvement of the Conan Doyles to Hawke.

He whistled. "I understand Houdini's concern — as a pressman — because if my colleagues got wind of all this, I'm afraid his campaign against fraud spiritualists would have floundered without the exposure of the Blackthornes. I know quite a lot about Marina and I can tell you she makes news. Fake or not, she has sold her psychic powers to many a seemingly shrewd person. Sir Arthur and Lady Doyle would just about complete her collection, so to speak. Unless they can be discredited they could certainly harm our tub-thumping friend. Is he going to be with us tonight at this seance given by . . . who did you say?" He took out his note book and started to write in it with a pencil (not an ordinary wooden one but a gold-plated patent contraption).

"The Reverend Septimus Carstairs, a simple cleric but enlightened and emancipated enough to be something of a spirit medium. He is my altar ego, if you will forgive the pun!" Holmes replied.

Hawke laughed, "Well, the reverend gentleman had better have something good up his cassock sleeve if he is going to impress the Blackthornes. But Holmes, what is the point of this seance, whatever its content?"

Holmes leant over, so that his prominent nose was close to the journalist's ear. Speaking quietly he said, "My dear Hawke, all will become clear to you and I am hoping the events of this evening will resolve the whole affair. All I ask is that you will report the seance and all that happens, including comments of those present, truthfully in your newspaper. The only other favour is that you keep up the deception concerning my demise in front of the Doyles and Blackthornes, to whom it will be a complete surprise. Houdini knows of the deception already and Watson, as my best and only friend, you must of course behave as if you had indeed been bereaved. Though not of course at the expense of the seance. That must go on, come what may."

Houdini was the next to arrive, soberly dressed in a dark and incredibly creased formal suit. He shook hands with Hawke. "Why Richard, how nice to see you again. Say did I ever thank you for that great story you wrote about my underwater escape from the Thames?"

Hawke smiled wryly, "I had an official thank-you note, I believe your wife signed it."

Houdini examined the fake news article. "Say that is a real good job! I don't pretend to understand exactly what you hope to do, Mr Holmes, but if you just want me to play up, I'm your man."

The Doyles and the Blackthornes arrived together, having evidently dined out as a foursome. After the usual niceties of greetings and introduction to Richard Hawke, the first test of Holmes's whole planned deception occurred.

Doyle was the first to glimpse the news story. He picked up the newspaper. "Good Lord, is this true, Sherlock Holmes is dead?" After being assured that it was so he said, "What a sad loss; a fine man, such a magnificent mind. Watson, my dear fellow you, as the one person really close to him, have my very deepest sympathy."

Lady Doyle looked sad, casting her eyes downward and saying little more than 'God rest his soul'. As for the Blackthornes, Marina was a good enough actress to appear sad but I thought I detected an expression of complete disinterest on the doctor's face.

Sir Arthur and Lady Conan Doyle, being the kindly and sensitive people that they are, were all for postponing the seance. "Do you really think Watson that we should go ahead under the circumstances?"

Lady Doyle added, "Yes, Doctor, maybe we should call it off as a mark of respect to your dear friend?"

Houdini took up his cue, "Oh come on, Sherlock Holmes wouldn't have wanted us to cry off on his account!"

They all turned to me to decide upon the matter and, in my turn, I transferred the responsibility to Holmes in his character of the benign cleric, "I really do believe that Holmes would have wanted us to go ahead, but I will be guided entirely by the Reverend Septimus Carstairs."

Holmes pressed the tips of his fingers together and pursed his lips in a fine ascetic manner. In a voice as unlike his own incisive tones as can be imagined, a voice which sounded as if it could have filled a cathedral, he announced, "Dear friends, I have given it some thought but I cannot believe that Sherlock

Holmes was the sort of man who would have wished us to change firmly made plans. After all, there is nothing frivolous in what we plan. I may be a spiritualist but I am also a man of God."

With this matter settled we shortly repaired to the seance room which had again been hired for the occasion. As instructed by the reverend gentleman, we seated ourselves in a semicircle, facing the medium who sat with that same small table before him. He asked if anyone wished to search his person, as had been done with the Blackthornes.

No one wished to do so, in fact Sir Arthur expressed a general feeling when he said, "If we cannot trust a vicar who can we trust, what?"

There was a little polite and sympathetic laughter to which Holmes responded by saying, "Dear brothers and sisters, I do not call you ladies and gentlemen because I feel that I know you too well." Then he put a hand to his lips as if to stifle a belch but, in fact, obviously from embarrassment. Again there was polite laughter and his muttered apology was scarcely necessary. Having recovered his composure he continued:

"As a man of God I have never quite understood the attitude of the Anglican Church toward spiritualism. Surely to make contact with the spirits of the dear departed is a good thing, especially for the bereaved and, indeed in so much as the very existence of the afterlife can be proven beyond doubt, I am of course a mere beginner in this field by comparison with some of you. I do not attempt the sort of manifestations that we witnessed and marvelled at last evening. But I do, once I have entered a suitable and receptive frame of mind which some of you might refer to as a trance, hear voices which can only be of spiritual origin. I converse with them and I feel sure that if I do receive such messages this evening, which I may or may not, that you will find this as fascinating as

I do. There is no need for the joining of hands, but I would appreciate absolute quiet and of course I would like the electric light to be extinguished."

Being nearest to the light switch I snapped it off so that the room was then in complete darkness. We sat in silence for perhaps ten minutes; certainly it seemed that long, before the cleric spoke: "I am beginning to hear voices, several voices, oh dear, they are all trying to speak to me at once. One of them says that his name is Charlie that he was once a soldier. Did anyone here know a Charlie who was in the British Army?"

It so happened that we had all known a soldier named Charlie at some time or other. Messages were repeated, purporting to be from Charlie, but which one of them was never quite clearly defined. Then a strange voice, obviously that of Septimus Carstairs lightly disguised, was heard, shouting such things as, "I want to go home. Why am I here?" and "I'm fed up with the lot of you!" The latter retort surprised us a little, but one had to admit that, compared to Marina's Wallace, Charlie was a mild spirit.

Another long silence ensued, which seemed to go on long enough to cause us concern as to the possibility that Carstairs had silently stolen away. It had been a most disappointing demonstration, with the medium simply speaking in his own and one other voice remarkably similar to his own, uttering a few phrases that seemed to have no particular significance.

The Doyles and Blackthornes shuffled in their seats with embarrassment with only Houdini and myself eventually remaining completely still and silent. At last someone spoke. The voice was that of Doctor Robert Blackthorne. "Perhaps you could try to contact the spirit of Sherlock Holmes?"

There were embarrassed tutting noises from the Doyles and Houdini said, "Sir, is that quite a nice thing to ask with Holmes so lately passed on and with his good friend Doctor Watson present?"

"Please, sir, do not worry on my account," I said, "such a message would comfort me; especially as I do not think my friend had any kind of conviction regarding the hereafter." I tailed off, hoping to have said the right thing as far as Holmes was concerned.

Evidently I had, for Carstairs said, "Thank you Doctor Watson, I will indeed try to contact your dear friend, though I imagine it is a little soon for any sort of spiritual presence to make itself known."

Another silence followed but mercifully, this time, it was a short one. Carstair's voice was heard again, "If the spirit of our dear brother Sherlock Holmes is present would it please make itself known to us by speaking or giving a sign?" He repeated this invitation two or three times until the whole thing began to be embarrassingly ridiculous. Only respect for the cloth kept our little circle intact.

Then, quite suddenly, a voice was heard, a very distinctive voice entirely unlike that of anyone in the room, in fact probably somewhat unlike that of anyone else upon this planet. It was beyond doubt the voice of Sherlock Holmes. It said, "You called upon me brother Septimus, so I am answering you. What do you wish to ask me?"

The agitated voice of Carstairs answered, "Dear brother Sherlock we, your friends, wish to know that you are safe and happy?"

Holmes's incisive tones replied, "I appear to be safe enough but far from happy as I have nothing to occupy my mind. Watson, dear old friend, I will await your arrival here with impatience but I warn you that there is no tobacco."

The eerie nature of the situation gripped me as much as anyone, even if I did know that it was not a spirit voice that spoke. No, it was the flesh-creeping drama with which Holmes the superb actor and mimic conducted this ghostly dialogue. The Doyles were greatly affected by it, I could sense, even in the dark. All attempts to observe any sort of silence were now cast aside through the dramatic shock of the situation.

Sir Arthur said quietly, "Praise be to God that you have been permitted to make contact with us my dear Holmes! You see Houdini there *is* life after death and it *is* possible for those on the other side to make contact with us!" Houdini grunted but said nothing.

Then at last Marina spoke, uttering the first words of doubt. "How do we know that this is the spiritual voice of Sherlock Holmes — or a spirit at all? I for one have never heard Mr Holmes's voice, to me this could be anyone, probably the old boy is a mimic."

Lady Doyle said, "Madam, you can take my word for it that we have indeed heard the voice of Sherlock Holmes. My husband and I have heard it so many times!"

I piped up, "That was Holmes

speaking; take it from me, I'd swear to it!" This I could safely do, knowing that it was indeed Holmes who had spoken.

It was Robert Blackthorne who struck the sourest note by saying, "Well, as Marina and I are unfamiliar with Sherlock Holmes's voice perhaps we too could be convinced by some other sign or manifestation?" There was a mocking note to his voice, as if he genuinely believed that Carstairs was a charlatan.

The vicar burbled and muttered, "I am just a simple cleric, I have served my purpose in allowing our dear brother to speak with you. I can say no more . . . I can . . . Oooh!"

Carstairs appeared to be suffering some sort of seizure. Then an incredible thing happened, almost as incredible to myself as to anyone. A faint, eerie blue light picked out the upper half of a figure seated at the table. But it was not the likeness of Carstairs that we saw but that of Sherlock Holmes! He sat as still as a statue, the faint blue glow just enough to make it clear to anyone who had ever seen him or his likeness that this was indeed the figure, or spectre, of Britain's most celebrated detective. The light, although faint, appeared to be directed from below, throwing into deep shadow every cadaverous ravine of his sharp-featured face. A mocking gleam seemed to emanate from his lustrous eyes.

At last he spoke, "It is good to see you again my dear Watson."

Possibly he spoke further words but these were drowned by a sudden scream from Marina. She all but shrieked, "It's true, there really *are* spirits! Oh Robert how wicked we have been to use trickery to falsify that in which we did not even believe! Sir Arthur, Lady Doyle, please forgive me. God forgive me . . . I have sinned!" Much to the amazed consternation of the Doyles she continued to make confessions concerning her activities as a spirit medium.

Holmes's voice eventually commanded me, "Turn on the light Watson, I think enough has now been heard, particularly by our friend Richard Hawke."

I switched on the light. This immediately made it obvious that Holmes was flesh and blood rather than spirit. Marina dropped her head into her hands as Doctor Blackthorne said, "Very clever Holmes, so you falsified your death as well as your spirit-self. You are as guilty as we are of deception."

Holmes replied, "Not quite, for I have no doubt that you had much to gain from making Sir Arthur and Lady Doyle believe that you could contact the spirits of those who had passed on — or is it over?"

Doyle then spoke. "We had been upon the point of making a large donation to Doctor Blackthorne to build a special spiritualist church."

"Sir Arthur, now do you not see that I had only your own good at heart when I claimed that you had been deceived so often and so easily by people like the Blackthornes?" Houdini broke in.

"Houdini, my faith in spiritualism and the ability of so many of the mediums we have encountered is not shaken in any way by the events of this evening. There are black sheep in every fold. As for you, Holmes, I am disappointed with your behaviour tonight. Was it kind to expose my wife and I to the shock of believing someone, for whom we had the greatest respect, to be dead?"

As the Blackthornes prepared to depart a voice was heard, the harsh voice that we had heard at the previous night's seance. "Death to Holmes. Death to Houdini!" Wallace was indeed displeased with recent events.

The Conan Doyles departed, much offended, and it was only then that I started to notice the actual mechanics of Holmes's deception or transformation from Septimus Carstairs to his own spirit. There beneath the table lay the cassock, long grey wig, thick spectacles and collar of the cleric.

"Where did that faint blue light come from Holmes?" He opened his jacket — for he had been wearing his normal attire beneath the cassock — and revealed to us a trumpet-shaped article; so constructed that it might be inserted at its tapered end into the top of his waistband. He explained, "It is a sort of battery-operated torch with, as you have seen, an eerie blue glow. It is manufactured specially for those who deceive the unsophisticated who so wish to believe. Earlier today I went to Green Street, just off Leicester Square, to visit the emporium of one Will Goldston, an enterprising gentleman who deals in apparatus for illusionists. He is well known to you of course, Mr Houdini, and I knew him from that occasion in 1918 when he was as interested as I was in the rather strange death of William Ellesworth Robinson, whose *nom de théâtre* was

Chung Ling Soo.

"You may remember, Watson, that Mr Goldston had an eccentric theory that Robinson had planned his own death which we were able to disprove. Mr Goldston supplied this little contraption which was just the icing on the cake.

"It was a brilliant touch, Mr Holmes, and I was shaken by it myself; even though I had some idea what you were up to." Houdini turned to Hawke, "You have enough to enable you to expose the Blackthornes?"

The journalist nodded. "Marina has held her last seance as far as what you would call the big-time is concerned. People of influence like the Doyles will never touch her again. As for your crusade, Mr Houdini, you have another notch to carve on your magic wand. I'll make it certain that every reader of the *Daily Falcon* is aware of this evening's incredible happenings, especially those outbursts from Marina."

All known rules of the Charing Cross Railway Hotel were broken for Sherlock

Holmes as we were served in the dining room with a meal of cold cuts and salad washed down with a bottle of claret. There were just the two of us, for Houdini, after expressing his profuse thanks, had departed to placate an irate wife and Hawke had sped to Fleet Street where the lights burned twenty-four hours a day. The snack was welcome and enabled us to replace the energies both physical and mental that had been consumed over the previous two days.

"Holmes, will you mind the return to notoriety which tomorrow's papers may bring you?" I asked my friend.

He smiled. "You are mistaken Watson, it will be Houdini who stars in tomorrow's dramatic disclosures. As Hawke and Houdini left us, they were deep in conversation and our American friend is very plausible. By tomorrow it will be he who exposed Marina. But that is as it should be, for he is a showman courting publicity at all times, whereas I am but an elderly retired investigator not requiring such limelight."

★ ★ ★

Rather to my surprise, I was able to entice Holmes to stay with me for a day or two before he returned to Fowlhaven. It was in my study at Finchley where I had made a fire despite the season, that we sat and studied the front-page item in the *Daily Falcon*. Holmes had been right, for it read: 'HOUDINI EXPOSES MEDIUM MARINA! That great American showman, the man who can escape from any restraint and make a live elephant disappear, last night exposed the so-called medium, Marina, by himself conjuring up the spirit of the famous Baker Street detective Sherlock Holmes at a seance attended by Sir Arthur and Lady Conan Doyle.'

There followed an account of those events of the night before which seemed to bear little likeness to what had actually occurred. It was evidently Houdini who had conceived the idea of the faked death report and the transformation of the bogus cleric into the enigmatic sleuth. The article finished with a puff for Houdini's latest appearances as a spook-buster and the forthcoming premiére of his moving picture *The Man from Beyond* in which he himself played the starring role.

Of course, Holmes had suspected that this would happen and had told me that it would. But even though I knew that he was untroubled by Houdini's seeming — to me — ingratitude I was still a little surprised by his unruffled calm. I said, as I felt I must, "Really Holmes, you have allowed Houdini to walk all over you!"

"Houdini has his problems, Watson, it is not all glory for him. I doubt if Sir Arthur will ever again give him more than a polite nod, however unreasonable that may sound."

"Just one last point upon this subject Holmes, what did you make of that coarse voice which threatened both

Houdini and yourself?" He did not laugh as I had half expected that he might.

"Yes, Wallace was furious was he not? I think Marina should go on the halls as the world's greatest ventriloquist, for that indeed she is. But she has a spitefulness, Watson, the last demonstration of which we might not yet have seen.

Holmes glanced at an envelope which stood propped up against an ornament upon the mantelpiece. "Ah, a woman's handwriting if I am not mistaken." He arose and without touching the envelope he investigated it with his prominent nose. "Traces of perfume. You are a dark horse Watson."

"If you must know everything Holmes, it is from that young woman to whom I loaned the money on the Embankment. No letter, just a five pound note in the envelope but obviously it is from her."

"Well there you are, Watson, your trust was not unfounded and you are as ever a good judge of character."

He glanced at me with an expression of — for him — great kindness but I thought I detected a twinkle in his eye.

As for Houdini, he was soon to return to the United States and would continue to make headlines almost daily for the next several years. He toured extensively in America giving a lecture entertainment almost entirely devoted to the exposure of fake mediums or spook crooks as he called them. He was loved, applauded, threatened and hated in turns. Then, towards the end of 1926, I learned that he had returned to a programme of escapology — as he called it — and magical entertainment. But early in November of the same year I read in the *Daily Falcon* that he had died, not from the hazardous effects of the underwater escape that was his featured item, but from peritonitis triggered by a blow to the stomach delivered to him by a student who had read that he could withstand such treatment without ill effect.

I was saddened by the news of his death. I had never quite known if I had liked Houdini or not but I had always recognized him as an exciting and enigmatic personality impossible to ignore. I corresponded with Sherlock Holmes upon the subject of Houdini's death. From what he wrote to me I gained the impression that he had admired — almost liked — Houdini. One of his letters ended, "One thing is certain Watson, we will not look upon his like again, yet I have a strong feeling that we have not heard the last of him."

Part Two

The Secret Box

It was upon a balmy midsummer evening in 1927 that a sudden banging upon my front door startled my reverie. There upon the doorstep stood Sherlock Holmes whose arrival had not been predicted by any sort of warning or message.

"Good evening my dear Watson, your lupins will soon be giving you a splendid show!" With bewildered mutterings I ushered him in, taking his hat and cane which were those one would normally associate with a country squire. His tweeds completed the picture; that of a gentleman suddenly called to the city upon urgent business.

I noted the overnight case that he had thrown down near my umbrella stand. I seated him in my favourite chair and plied him with coffee. I first welcomed him and then asked him, "How many nights do you intend to stay?"

"Ah, you have noted the Gladstone? Well, that will rather depend upon the outcome of a meeting which we have tomorrow at the Ritz Hotel."

"Please, Holmes, elucidate as soon as you have refreshed and composed yourself."

"Watson, I do not undertake investigations any more as you well know, unless they are of great personal or national interest. But that which has torn me away from my rustication in Sussex is really by way of being the settlement of unfinished business. Remember friend Houdini whose spiritualistic and theatrical activities were so rudely interrupted by his death last Halloween? Well his wife, Mrs Beatrice Houdini, wishes to consult me concerning some aspects of his demise untimely. That death was, as you will remember, part of a scenario which he might have dictated himself. He went out in a blaze of publicity."

"When did you hear from the lady?"

"She wrote to me some weeks ago, before taking ship for Southampton, but she assumed the date of her arrival and establishment at the Ritz. The rendezvous is for tomorrow but I received the letter but hours ago; so the lady is somewhat less businesslike than her husband. I apologize for this sudden intrusion but time has not been on my side. You will, I trust, be able to arrange for your practice to be managed by others for a day or two?"

This last remark surprised me because when last we had met, perhaps a year before, I had been all but retired, having but recently been thrust back into medical activity through force of circumstances. Reading my mind, as always, he said, "The iodine stain on your left hand tells its own story. I'll have another cup of that which passes with you for coffee. That you have run out of your usual brand and fallen back upon bottled Empire tells me also that you have been more than busy, for you were always well organized in such matters. By the way, have you quite eliminated the mice from your spare bedroom? I would hate to be kept awake by their scamperings."

Despite thirty-five years of exposure to his methods he never ceased to amaze me. I had not, until very recently, been troubled by mice in my house; only one room being affected and the matter resolved.

Almost apologetically, he explained, "I'm afraid I took a glance at the side of your house before I raised your knocker. Call it force of habit or just plain curiosity, as you wish. I noticed that you had erected a garden shed — since my last visit to you — of the kind which almost always attracts the attention of the common fieldmouse. The shed was immediately below the window to your spare bedroom which has a section of trellis reaching from the ground to the sill. I noted the marks left by our little friends as they transferred their attention from shed to trellis and trellis to windowsill. But don't worry, Watson, the fieldmouse is a cleaner animal than his indoor cousin but at certain times of the year not averse to an indoor life."

"Holmes, it cost me several pounds paid to an artisan who professed expert knowledge to rid me of the mice. From what you have told me it would have been so much easier for me to simply move the shed — and cheaper!"

"Don't forget my present rural surroundings," my friend responded.

We talked for several hours about old times, great days and remarkable events. Indeed, it was well past midnight when I showed him to my mouse-free spare bedroom. On the following morning, I rose rather later than usual. Washing, shaving and dressing hastily, I descended to my dining room where I found Holmes, immaculate and freshly shaved, sitting with a coffee pot and the remains of a substantial breakfast.

"Doctor, I hope you will forgive

me for taking such advantage of your hospitality. I took the liberty of admitting your daily woman when she arrived."

Then, as if on cue in a theatrical piece, Mrs Morgan, my domestic, entered — all smiles — bearing a fresh supply of toast and another pot of hot coffee.

Holmes beamed at her. "Bless you my dear Mrs Hudson, you are really quite spoiling me!"

Mrs Morgan simpered, "It's a pleasure Mr 'Olmes, I always followed the accounts of your carrying-on in *The Strand*. At least, my Albert did, an' 'ee used to tell me all about them!"

Holmes bowed his head and then with a gesture towards myself said, "You have the good doctor to thank for all that and, of course, Sir Arthur Conan Doyle."

She simpered again and, as she left the room, she whispered to me, "Such a nice gentleman, but why does 'e call me 'Udson?" I shrugged, feeling it better not to try to explain. As I partook of my breakfast, we discussed the course that the next few hours would take.

"Watson, our appointment with Mrs Beatrice Houdini is for midday at the Ritz. I suggest that we take the underground railway. If we leave here at about ten-thirty of the clock we should be in good time." Unmindful that I was still eating, he brought forth his pipe and pouch, soon filling my dining room with clouds of blue smoke and an atmosphere strangely reminiscent of our old rooms at Baker Street.

As I drank my coffee, I asked a few questions. "You have told me why you have decided to see Mrs Houdini, Holmes, but I wonder if you have considered just what her present problems might be?"

"I imagine the lady has shared my own feeling that there was something not quite right about the circumstances of her husband's death. That is if you discount the possibility of her rendezvous suggestion being merely a friendly gesture."

Perhaps, on reflection, I said, a little too quickly, "I do indeed discount that possibility. Mrs Houdini showed very little desire for our company during her last visit to London."

Holmes chuckled. "I couldn't have put it better myself, Watson."

The half-hour spent travelling by underground proved uneventful enough to allow us to indulge in gossip concerning the events in our lives that had occurred since our last meeting. Holmes told me about one or two events in Fowlhaven that had involved him in assisting the one local representative of law and order. "I do not seek to involve myself, Watson, but then neither I imagine do you any more wish to concern yourself with the health of the populace. You are a humanitarian and, whilst I would not apply that term to myself, there are times when I can hardly refuse to use my talents — such as they are."

There was time to spare when we arrived at Green Park, so we took a stroll along Piccadilly to gaze at the place where once had stood Maskelyne's Egyptian Hall Theatre; the scene of an adventure in which we had both participated so many years before, when the game had been well and truly afoot.

Picking up my own thoughts, Holmes said, "The times change, as do tastes Watson, but not perhaps always for the better." I gazed at the shopfront, which replaced the previous stately columns, and nodded my agreement.

As we entered the huge residential lounge of the Ritz, we at once perceived the lady we were seeking. She was handsomely gowned and coiffured; though clearly middle-aged. Beatrice Houdini had never been a great beauty but, as of yore, she still presented an attractive appearance; amplified perhaps by the fact that her dark hair was now shot with startlingly white streaks. She inclined her head in recognition as we neared her. "Mr Holmes and dear Doctor Watson too! Say, can I call you Doc, Harry always did? It is good of you both to give me your time." We both made suitable polite rejoinders and I made no comment about being called Doc.

She had a somewhat younger woman with her, also expensively gowned and introduced to us as, 'my companion, Daisy'. We sat upon a long sofa opposite the two women and divided from them by a low coffee table upon which were cocktail glasses. Mrs Houdini asked us if we wanted any refreshment, "A Martini, or a Manhattan?"

We settled for a pot of tea which was brought for us by a waiter who bore also replacement cocktails for Beatrice and Daisy. Niceties over, Mrs Houdini got down to brass tacks. "Mr Holmes, I want to remind you of the details of the events that led directly to my poor dear Harry's death last fall. Peritonitis was the official cause of his death, following a ruptured appendix; the result of a series of blows to his abdomen, delivered by some fool student from the McGill University."

Holmes interrupted, "I seem to have read that this occurred in Mr Houdini's dressing room at the theatre in Montreal?"

"Yes, this young guy came into the dressing room with some other folk from the university where Harry had just delivered a lecture — as if he didn't have enough on his plate what with the show — on spiritualism. Harry was reclining on a couch, reading some letters; typically answering his visitor's foolish questions in a rather absent-minded manner. Everyone in the room was hanging on his every word. It's a pity he wasn't hanging on theirs as it happens! You see this student, Whitehead, asked Harry if it was true that he could withstand hard punches in the stomach. Harry said that it was so and evidently this young guy asked if he could put this to the test. Well, Harry was so absorbed with what he was reading that he would have said yes or no to anything they said. If only it had been no! Before anyone could stop him this guy had landed two or three sharp punches on Harry's belly. I tell you, those punches would have rocked a prize fighter. Of course, Harry made light of it but I could see that he had been badly hurt. I tell you, I could have killed this guy, even if it wasn't quite his fault.

"Harry had a doctor look him over and he diagnosed the ruptured appendix. Instead of going straight to a hospital he carried on with the show that night and not only that but with the tour as well. He ignored all my pleas and, by the time we got to Detroit, anyone could see that he was in agony. A couple more shows and Harry had to give in. Three surgeons combined to remove his appendix but when it was out they told me that the poisons had been going through his bloodstream for too long to hold out any hope of recovery. He was a fighter, sure, but he died in my arms at one-thirty on the morning of October the thirty-first."

I whistled softly, "Good Lord, that means that he survived for a week that which as a doctor I would normally expect to kill within hours!"

Holmes, who had been quiet for rather a long time said, "So, the Great Houdini was a man of mystery to the last, leaving this world at Halloween. The drama of such a seasonal departure would not have displeased his sense of theatre but I find it sad that a man who had survived so many duels with death should die through such a preventable incident. Dear lady, whilst I sympathize I fail to see what I can do that would be of any help to you at this stage."

Beatrice Houdini dropped her bomb-shell. "Mr Holmes, I believe that Harry was murdered!"

"What?" I gasped, as I leapt to my feet, only to be restrained and reseated by Holmes, who spoke calmly. "Such a thought crossed my mind when first I read of his demise. The circumstances were bizarre and followed, as I recall, a number of other suspicious accidents. However, it is late in the day for accusations."

The lady emptied her glass and signalled to the waiter to refill it before saying, "I am not of course suggesting that this student killed Harry deliberately, it's more the thought that someone might have put him up to it in the hope that the result would be just as it was."

"But surely, had Houdini not been distracted, events would have taken a different turn?" I exclaimed.

She said, "Sure Doc, it would then have been just one in a series of incidents which were, I believe, inspired by someone who hoped, or knew, that sooner or later a fatal accident would occur."

Holmes asked if he might smoke and, that permission having been granted, lit a cigar of a kind which was the nearest means of sampling strong tobacco in female company. We observed the irritatingly slow ritual in which he removed the band, then cut and lit the cigar. At last he spoke:

"To my mind what you have said bears some substance. Your husband had enemies, professional rivals and, of course, many among the psychic-fraudsters yet I find it hard to believe that any of these people would take their dislike or envy so far as to commit murder. Financial gain is quite another thing and is certainly one of the commoner motives for homicide. Who benefited from Houdini's death from a financial point of view?"

"His brother, Dash; he got the act and a few minor gratuities. The Library of Congress got most of his huge and valuable book collection and his surviving sister got a small amount in cash and bonds but the actual bulk of his estate was willed to me and

Mr Doyle. I assure you, I didn't kill Harry."

The lady spoke frankly, a woman who obviously put all her cards on the table, as her next statement illustrated. "You see, I had a number of insurance policies taken out on Harry quite aside from the principal life policy which he had set up himself. Harry knew about these, except for one of them. You know, in the United States you can take out a policy on anyone, for anything, without the person concerned even having to know. After a number of suspicious accidents, I took out an extra policy with a small company who was willing to issue it. To cut everything to the quick, Mr Holmes, I will get half a million dollars if I can prove that Harry was murdered."

Holmes and I were both considerably shaken, although I believe he managed to conceal his surprise better than I. He considered the glowing end of his cigar before he spoke, "I take it madam that we can have your assurance that you would have made, nay did make, every effort to prevent any of these suspicious accidents from becoming fatal?"

She smiled; she had a way of doing this without opening her mouth. I soon deduced that this was in an effort to conceal rather prominent front teeth.

"Mr Holmes, Houdini was worth a great deal more to me alive than any half-a-million bucks. We lived high on the hog, carried people with us everywhere to wait upon us hand and foot, stayed at the very best hotels and dined at the finest restaurants. Aside from this, there was a kudos attached to being the wife of the Great Houdini that being his widow just does not carry. But picking up that five-hundred-thousand dollars could go a long way to soothing me down."

Sherlock Holmes smiled, almost kindly, "Dear lady, can you not take your suspicions to the police?"

"Ah, they don't want to know for they suspect me of being after publicity.

Why I don't know because I've got no fish to peddle!"

"Are there no private investigators in America who might be happy to help you?"

Holmes's enquiry produced a derisive reply. "A New York private dick would cost a fortune and fail to deliver. You, I know, you I trust for heaven's sake. Please help me, Mr Holmes, you are my only chance."

I admit that I had half expected Holmes to mutter something to the effect that he was far too busy with his bees. I thought that he then might politely beg our leave and be unmoved by the display of tears which I fully expected would follow such a step. Imagine then my surprise when I heard him say, "If I do make some enquiries, I will expect you to be completely frank with me Mrs Houdini. Moreover, again if I do, it will not be on account of your insurance policy but rather to see justice done. There are aspects of the affair that interest me and I feel that matters current and involving me not long before Houdini's death were never completely resolved."

She brightened. "You won't regret it Shamus."

Although I did not know the meaning of this name I suspect Holmes did, for he said, "My name, Mrs Houdini, is Sherlock Holmes and, as for matters of finance, I have a set scale of fees which does not vary save where I choose to omit it altogether. But, if it is necessary for Watson and I to travel to the United States, you may settle our day-to-day expenses, which despite our temperate ways and frugal habits are likely to prove expensive."

She was delighted and hinted darkly at a locked box which Houdini had left her with the instruction that it should not be opened until fifty years had followed his death. "If you stay in New York for a day or two I can introduce you to everyone who loved him, feared him, or just plain hated his guts and, believe me, Sherlock there were a lot of those! I'll put you up at a nice hotel near my home everything paid for and, of course, you can go back with me next week on the *New Mayflower* first-class."

To my utter amazement, Holmes agreed to all of this on behalf of us both without the nicety of prior consultation with myself. Sometimes I think he takes me too much for granted.

As she walked with us to the lobby, Beatrice Houdini slipped her hand around my right biceps and said, "We'll have fun on board Doc, never fear!" It was but forty minutes after midday, yet she was not quite sober. This I found very sad but I noted that her companion seemed to have the situation well in hand saying, "Beatrice, come on, time for a quick nap before lunch."

On the journey back to my home Sherlock said, "I knew that I could depend on your participation in one last adventure Watson: *Sherlock Holmes and the Houdini Enigma*. How might that title attract your readers and gain you another fat cheque from *The Strand*?"

* * *

Despite the confines of an ocean liner, Holmes became adept at avoiding too much contact with Beatrice and Daisy on the voyage. He had a great many excuses concerning dances, functions and whist drives which were not only convincing in themselves but delivered with a firmness that made them unquestioned. In fact, I almost felt that he had overdone it a bit, as I for one would have welcomed the odd diversion. As it was, however, we spent a lot of time in our adjoining cabins with Holmes either studying the small print on the Acme Insurance Policy with which Mrs Houdini had provided him or playing mournfully upon his violin. He had thought to bring a vast supply of black shag, so his cabin soon filled with a fog reminiscent of

Baker Street in November. Indeed, on one occasion, this smoke issued forth when his cabin door opened and was responded to with a ship's fire drill.

The Hotel Brownstone was near enough to Beatrice Houdini's home to be convenient yet far enough from it for comfort. We had a large room between us which could have accommodated two more persons, having four beds in all. We settled in quite comfortably and then visited Beatrice Houdini's home on the second day of our arrival.

She gave a small dinner gathering for us. The guests included Houdini's brother, Theodore Hardeen — Dash as Houdini had always called him. Whilst he bore quite a likeness to his brother, Theo Hardeen struck me as being far less Aryan in appearance and, of course, a few inches taller. He showed us press books and publicity items relating to the days before the turn of the century when he and Harry were a double act: The Brothers Houdini. But Holmes seemed to find these items of less interest than the album of family photographs which Theodore had also brought with him. Taking his lens from a vest pocket, Holmes surveyed the serried ranks of old sepia photographs depicting the Weiss family; mother Cecelia who had the same broad forehead as her son Harry and the father, the Rabbi Weiss with his neat beard and prayer shawl. The several brothers and sisters all resembled each other rather more than they did Harry himself.

Holmes asked Theo if he considered that his brother had made a lot of enemies. He considered carefully before he answered. "Well, my friend, I'll tell you, Harry was the sort of guy who made a lot of enemies among the small-time operators who tried to emulate his success. They were annoyed because he had taken their age-old business from the fairgrounds and with it put himself into the big time show business. In their envy they never seemed to take into account that he was different to them in that he had class. Hell, he had a lot more class than I got and I'm no bum. They knew how he worked and tried to do the same things but couldn't understand why they couldn't break in. There was only one Houdini and if anyone tried to bother him seriously he would put them down with ridicule and lawsuits. If that didn't stop them, he and I would beat them up in some dark alley."

I was rather aghast at this statement. "I say, a bit steep that, what?" But Hardeen only laughed, "Doc, you've got to remember that Harry and I was raised in the ghetto and came up the real hard way. We never got nothin' we didn't fight for and that habit kind of stuck with us. Harry and I worked our way up through carnivals, side-shows, wagon outfits and burlesque through to big time vaudeville, I can remember a time when Harry worked in the street and I had to pass round the hat. He had paid his dues, earned his place in the sun and was determined to keep others out, especially Johnny-come-latelys who had not even worked the dumps like we did."

"What made you cash-in on being his brother rather than establish yourself in some other type of business?" asked Holmes.

Theodore Hardeen's eyes narrowed. "We figured that if anyone was going to even begin to rival Harry it might as well be me. I was the *other* Houdini as far as bookers were concerned. It kept out any other really serious contender and the money stayed in the family. Harry was a great guy, a good friend and a wonderful brother but you could easily fall out with him unless you went along with his quaint ways. Say, Bess, do you remember that night about thirty years ago when he took us both onto a bridge at midnight and made us raise our right hands and swear always to be true to him, like we were in court or church or something?"

"Can I ever forget and would he ever let me?"

"Me too but that's the kind of guy he was; you just couldn't refuse him anything. He was generous — at times at least. Life is dull without him. He left me the bulk of his show properties you know but I still work the act I have always had. For instance, there is a milk churn which he used to escape from after it had been filled with milk and he had been locked into it. Trouble is, it's too small for me to get into, let alone out of. Most of the stuff is like that — made to measure — but I'll keep it all as long as I live out of respect."

"You were not there were you when Houdini received those blows to the stomach?" prompted Holmes.

"Nah, I was playing some tank town in the south. Of course, I went to the hospital a few days later; just as soon as I knew it was serious and not just a publicity story. At first I thought he'd shrug it off and be out of there before I even got there. He seemed indestructible, you know. He

138

suffered a thousand injuries in his time — from ruptured kidneys to broken bones. Only a week or two before he died he had fractured an ankle doing the water-torture cell escape."

Holmes's interest increased. "What were the circumstances?"

"Well, the thing was a huge rectangular tank, glass-fronted. Houdini was lowered into the water head-downwards by means of a set of ankle stocks worked by a pulley. The stocks got jerked just a little too erratically at the wrong moment. With the pain in his ankle to contend with he was lucky to get out alive. Of course, the publicity involves two guys with hatchets standing by to break the glass if he was in trouble. That satisfied the authorities but in fact they never could have got him out in time. Like I say, that night he was lucky."

"I imagine the assistant who pulled the pulley rope was well trained?" asked Holmes.

"Well, yes, either Jim Collins or Jim

Vickery would usually do it but, as it happens, they were both off with some kind of influenza. A new guy pulled him up and that is why it happened."

Holmes was more than interested now. "Who was this new guy, as you call him?"

The reply seemed to interest him even more. "Oh, someone called Zoltan I believe, don't know his other name. He seemed to shape up well at rehearsal but on the show he just pulled too hard, too soon, often happens like that."

"What happened to this Zoltan?"

"I don't know, he didn't stick around long; got tired of being bawled out by Harry. He was a Hunky, they are always fiery tempered."

"Hunky . . . you mean he was a Hungarian. Are you sure?"

"I should know, we are all Hungarians in the Weiss family; even if we are naturalized Americans."

Later, Holmes asked me what I made of Hardeen.

"He expresses himself in a rather

similar way to his brother, though he has even less education. He is of course taller than Houdini and, although there is a likeness, it is rather superficial."

Holmes nodded, "The likeness, such as it is, appears to be from the mother's side of the family. Did you study carefully those old family photographs that he showed to us?"

"As carefully as the time allowed. I noticed that they appeared to be a typically close-knit immigrant family."

"Exactly, did you notice how closely the brothers and sisters resembled each other, with the one exception, that of Houdini himself? The others carry characteristics of both parents but Houdini, please observe Watson, has a likeness to her but none whatever to the good Rabbi Weiss."

He opened a small portfolio and took from it a photograph of Houdini as a very young man, stiffly posed between his parents. I studied it and had to agree. "What do you deduce from that Holmes?"

He pondered, charging his pipe before he replied. "It may have no meaning whatever, for this other influence which his features, indeed even his bearing and general manner, present may mean that he rather favours a grandparent or even a great-grandparent in appearance. He could be a throwback to an even more distant relative."

Beatrice Houdini's house, number 67 Payson Avenue, we found to be in something of a turmoil. She had only recently moved there from the family home that she and Harry had occupied at 113th Street. There were crates, piles of books, cardboard boxes and pieces of magical equipment everywhere. She apologized for the disorder: "I'm getting rid of all this junk as fast as I can by donating, selling and just plain giving it away. Daisy and I want to move out of New York eventually. I'd like a real home, I've lived in a museum for thirty years."

She introduced us to a Mr Bernard Ernst, as 'Harry's attorney'. Mr Ernst was a dapper man, neatly dressed, balding with a spruce, clipped moustache. He spoke in the tones of a cultured American. He was amazed when told, in confidence, the reason for Holmes's investigations.

"Good Lord, I feel sure you can eliminate any thought of foul play! Harry was a God-fearing man, always kind to others and so respectful to women and his elders. He was fond of animals and worshipped his mother. He was in fact a saintly man, Mr Holmes; why on earth would anyone want to harm him?"

My friend illustrated to me how well he could control his true feelings and beliefs when he said, "Quite so Mr Ernst, but I just want to put Mrs Houdini's mind at rest. Are you quite sure that you can think of nobody who might bear him a grudge?"

When Ernst referred to Houdini as a saintly man I did not dare catch Sherlock Holmes's eye for I knew that certain thoughts must be passing through both our minds. Ernst then proceeded to rattle off fully a dozen people who had never wished the showman any good, mostly rival illusionists; De Biere, Goldin, Cirnoc, Kleppini, they varied between the illustrious and the all-but-unknown names. Then there was Doctor Wilson, editor of the *Sphinx Magazine*; a man of unblemished character short of a dislike for the man whom he considered an upstart. A writer, Clinton Burgess, could have held a grudge over a book contract and there were other names that we did not recognize. Following this, Ernst reeled off a list of magic clubs and societies and finished by mentioning the entire Imperial German Government of the immediate pre-war era.

We did not mention the murder clause in the Acme Insurance policy, having been asked not to do so by Beatrice, even in conversation with this, her late husband's lawyer.

Mrs Houdini made our investigations

rather easier by holding a dinner party to which she had invited six or seven of Houdini's friends and colleagues. She had herself cooked an excellent meal; the main course being roast pork. She announced to the company in general, "I miss dear Harry so but I can't tell you how wonderful it is to be able to eat and serve whatever I like! Harry was not orthodox but he did draw the line at roast pork. I'm a Catholic you know and that applies to my tastes too."

The dinner guests had not been informed of the true purpose of our presence, with us being introduced as, "two of Harry's friends from England, the famous detective Sherlock Holmes and his sidekick, Doc Watson!" Holmes's exploits were as celebrated in America as they were at home and he was certainly the lion of the evening. As most of my readers will know, the Americans have more relaxed ways than ours, even where a fairly formal dinner party is concerned. For example, there is no observance of the age-old British custom of the ladies withdrawing to leave the gentlemen to their port. Instead everyone repairs to the lounge for coffee; an arrangement far more to my liking. As we drank the milky beverage from blue china cups we were, I feel sure, able to gain more information through simple conversation than would have been possible had our mission been made known.

One of the guests, Joseph Dunninger, was a rival magical showman who spoke well of Houdini which was scarcely surprising in the presence of Beatrice. He was a distinguished-looking man, formally dressed for an American as far as his evening dress was concerned. He spoke with a studied tone, rather like a man who had come from lowly origins but had taken on the speech and manners of those that he wished to emulate. He was quite unlike Houdini in this particular, for Harry had never seemed ashamed of his rough speech.

"You knew Harry of course, Mr

Holmes, but did you ever see him perform?" asked Dunninger.

Holmes shook his head. "No and this makes it hard for me to visualize that which made him so celebrated. I have spoken to those who have inferred that he simply took some old fairground deceptions and polished them for a theatre audience."

I could see that Holmes was baiting Dunninger, in order to extract something of value to us.

"My dear sir, you oversimplify! There is a basic truth in that but he did more than polish those old gimcracks; he improved them out of all recognition and above all he presented them with a sort of dynamic charm. He was dramatic, he was exciting, but above all he was charismatic. With Harry it was all in the pre-sen-tation. (Dunninger had this trick of elongating his words, as if working to a distant gallery.) For instance, a few years ago Harry appeared at the New York Hippodrome. It's a huge house, a really big theatre. His music played, it was a Sousa march and, try to imagine this Mr Holmes, out onto that enormous stage stepped Harry Houdini, a man of less-than-average height, ever so slightly bow-legged and wearing a tuxedo suit that looked like he'd slept in it. With one hand held behind his back, like Napoleon in reverse, he walked to the centre, placed one foot onto the footlights, leant forward and turned onto that audience the most beautiful smile in the whole history of show business. He was not just a great showman, the guy was charismatic! That was the real secret of Harry Houdini."

I glanced at Mrs Houdini and noticed a tear in her eye. I'll be frank and say that this far I had considered her to be rather a cold fish but I now realized that Beatrice Houdini really did care. As for the rest of the guests, they nodded wisely.

One of them, a John Mulholland, added, "He was a bit of a contradiction was Harry. Off stage he could be just as charming as Joe has described. But sometimes he could be just the opposite; it depended how the mood took him. I think Bess will forgive me for saying that mood swings were part of Harry's character." He looked a little bit uncomfortable as if he had caught a gleam in Beatrice Houdini's eye, then continued, "Of course he was always kind to those less fortunate than himself. He gave plenty of time to beginners in magic and if you were getting up a collection for charity you could always depend upon his generosity."

"Did the mood swings that you refer to mean that he made a number of enemies?" I enquired.

Holmes glared at me as if to say, "Watson, don't make our enquiries so obvious." I realized though, almost as soon as I had spoken, that I had overplayed my hand.

Mulholland, however, did not take my question as being unusual. "Doctor

Watson, all great showmen, all great magicians, in fact, all great men make enemies. They don't have to do much more than succeed in order to gain them. But there are a couple of Harry's professional colleagues, straight-shooters at that who were scarcely crazy about him. Take Horace Goldin, for example, a lovely guy, a great magician and very inventive. He made a fortune out of sawing women in half — why that illusion is perhaps the most famous theatrical draw in the vaudeville field that we are ever likely to see. The demand from managements was so great at one point that Horace had to hire at least half a dozen other illusionists to tour road companies while he presented it himself in the prime venues. Servais Le Roy and Harry Jansen, for example; these guys were big names already but happy to glean some of the pickings from the sawing illusion. But Horace is a big gambler, he loses fortunes as fast as he makes 'em! Right now he is back to playing the variety houses in your country Mr Holmes . . . even plays picture houses in between the movies. I tell ya he needs the dough."

I could see that Holmes was anxious to gain information of a more pertinent nature without making this too obvious. Almost casually he asked, "I wonder why he disliked Harry Houdini?"

Bess gave a sharp glance in Dunninger's direction, so I imagine the reply that Holmes received was milder than it might have been had Mrs Houdini not been present.

"Oh it was a storm in a teacup really. You see, Houdini was already famous when Horace was still making his way. Goldin thought that once whilst they were in Martinka's magic shop that Harry treated him with less than the respect that he figured he deserved. Afterwards, when Horace became a big name also he would leave a room if Harry entered it and would refer to him as Dime Museum Harry."

"Goldin is a nobody, not good

enough to clean Harry's boots!" Bess interrupted. There was a gentle murmur of dissent but nobody commented. Dunninger hastily changed his subjective comment. "There is also De Biere. Now there is a highly respected guy and a consummate artist. But Harry latterly spoke rather harshly about him. I don't know the reason."

"Arnold De Biere invested in one of Harry's movies," Bess chimed in. "It lost money and Harry lost a fortune. De Biere lost some money too, but he went into the deal with his eyes wide open. He is just a cry baby. Show business is a gamble. God knows I can vouch for that. Harry was always bold in his ventures and if he lost out he would pick himself up and start over."

Joseph Dunninger was the first to take his leave, departing, it seemed to me, as soon as he decently could. He was effusive in his farewells to Bess but she was icily polite. He turned to Holmes as he departed, "I'm starting a new radio show soon, Mr Holmes. The formula will be as before, where I show a trick to a different celebrity each week. I'd like to include you if you are still in town. It would be great to bill myself as the man who fooled Sherlock Holmes."

My friend smiled and nodded politely but after Dunninger had departed he murmured to me, "Watson, I wonder if he has considered the possibility that after appearing on his wireless entertainment I might be able to have some cards printed to the effect that I am the only man not to be fooled by the Great Dunninger?"

Other guests lingered longer. The youngest among them, who was little more than a boy, told us that his professional name was Milbourne Christopher. When I enquired what his off-stage name was he said, "Christopher Milbourne, I just changed them around. I got into magic after seeing Horace Goldin from the back of the gallery in Baltimore when I was five years old. He really inspired me and I'd like to present a show just like his. But I have another ambition, to be a famous writer and what I would really like to do is work on a biography of Houdini. That really would make a great book."

Beatrice Houdini breathed heavily. "Harold Kellock is working on Harry's biography, under my supervision. Say kid, why don't you go write about Horace Goldin if you admire him so much?" Christopher blushed and murmured some apologetic and placating words, then melted into the background.

Bess turned to Daisy and enquired in a stage whisper, "Who invited *him*?"

"I certainly didn't!" Daisy hissed. "I think he came with Dunninger — pity he didn't leave with him!"

Soon the magicians present were showing each other card tricks whilst Bessie held court with their wives. Holmes and I repaired to the back garden where we could smoke our pipes without giving offence to the ladies. "Watson, there would appear to be no shortage of rivals and those who disliked Houdini for one reason or another but so far I cannot imagine any that we have met as wishing him dead," commented Holmes.

"How about this Horace Goldin that Dunninger spoke of?"

"The man is famous, almost as famous as Houdini himself. He would have a lot to lose. No, there is a great deal of ground to cover, I'll be bound before we gain even the whisper of a lead in this affair. Moreover, it is extremely likely that we are on a fool's errand and that no foul play is involved. And yet . . . "

I caught the gleam in his gimlet eyes. I could tell that Sherlock Holmes was intrigued and intended to continue an open-minded series of enquiries.

The following day Beatrice Houdini invited us to visit the New York film studio where, she told us, Harry made a couple of his movies. I found that this diversion was most interesting and entertaining but I could see that

Holmes wondered a little at her motive. None the less he did not question the purpose of our visit and seemed also to be intrigued with the business of making a movie. We were taken into a structure, rather like an aeroplane hangar where scenery had been erected, before which actors played their roles. Between us and all of this there existed a vast collection of paraphernalia in the form of floodlights and a very large moving picture camera upon a wheeled tripod, plus a number of other contraptions the purpose for which I had no inkling. After we had spent an interesting hour watching the director coaxing the actors and actresses through their performances, Bessie took us to the office of a Mr Burton King, who she introduced to us as the man who directed for Harry in *The Man from Beyond*.

King was an impressive, active-seeming man of distinguished appearance. We sat in his office over the inevitable cup of coffee as he told us something of his association with Houdini.

"We shot most of the footage in New Jersey and combined it with some location stuff shot in Hollywood and at Niagara Falls." Holmes was interested in the need for these location scenes.

"We could never set up a big outdoor scene in this studio but it's cheaper to get scenes shot in California and then back-project them onto a big screen and have the actors work in front of it, reshooting the whole thing. A lot more economical than sending a whole bunch of actors out to Hollywood. Why you'd need to keep them up there in hotels, where here they go home nights. Saves a fortune. Of course there are companies in Hollywood to whom money is no object, they waste it on all manner of things. They'll put people on their payroll at the drop of a hat, just because they have some special knowledge or claim to fame, so to speak."

He picked up a handful of photographs and spread them on the desk in front of us. "See this guy here?" He pointed to a figure in a group of four actors. The man indicated was wearing, like the others, the sort of clothing that one would associate with that worn on the great prairies. He had a weather-beaten face and sported a hard stetson-type hat. King continued, "His name is Al Jennings for present purposes but he claims to be the famous outlaw Jesse James."

I was astonished, having believed that James had been shot in the back by a man called Bob Ford; the London newspapers having made much of this fact a few years earlier. I mentioned this, but King said, "Well, that is what everyone believed, but according to Jennings another guy got shot and buried, believed by everyone to be Jesse. I tell ya Doc, this guy Jennings knows so much about Jesse that it doesn't seem possible that it ain't him! You can ask him about Jesse's background and associates and exploits until the cows come home and get convincing answers, all of which get substantiated by enquiries. One of the big companies have signed him up, to play Jesse in a movie. In fact, they are making enquiries and discreet negotiations right now, to be sure that if they reveal him as Jesse, he doesn't get arrested before the picture is finished. I think it will be OK. I don't believe there is any state that wants Jesse for anything after so long."

Holmes was intrigued, I could tell, and his usually sharp eyes glistened with amusement. He turned to me. "Imagine what might happen, Watson, if it was decided to make a moving picture about the late lamented Professor Moriarty and an individual presented himself, claiming to be the professor, with a convincing story to the effect that he did not in fact perish at the Reichenbach Falls?"

"But his death was proven beyond doubt."

"So was mine, Watson, so was mine."

I could give no answer to this but King obviously found Holmes's words both amusing and intriguing. "Say Mr Holmes, would you consider playing yourself in a movie?"

Holmes made light of this. "William Gillette does it better and looks more like me than I do."

This was all but true and I entertained King with a retelling of the events of some twenty years earlier in which Holmes had capitalized upon the likeness between himself and Gillette and which I had titled in my mind as 'The Adventure of the Eminent Thespian'.

Burton King then placed another photograph upon the table, this one of a much earlier vintage than those depicting Jennings and others. The picture was a sepia-toned, whole-plate studio portrait of a man of some thirty years dressed in what I can only describe as formal Western attire. He adopted the stiff pose required from a long exposure and his right hand was placed upon the hilt of a huge Colt revolver which rested in a holster at his waist, his jacket raised slightly to accommodate this pose.

"This is an authentic portrait of Jesse James, taken at about the time when he quit being an outlaw and took to family life," said King. "If you compare it with those stills of Jennings I think you will see why his claim to be Jesse has been widely accepted."

Holmes laid the most graphic photograph of the group and the authentic picture of Jesse James side by side. His eyes closed down to sharpen his vision and he made comparison. "Allowing for the passing of a decade or two there is a more than significant likeness. Not only are the features in general extremely similar but the ears in particular," Holmes said, at length.

I understood why he made this emphasis, because many a case of mistaken identity has ultimately been resolved through a study of these appendages. Medical authorities have assured criminologists that no two pairs of ears are exactly alike.

"We must assume that no record of James's fingerprints exist, otherwise the matter would have been resolved beyond doubt." Holmes took his lens from an inside jacket pocket and scanned the pictures again with its aid. Then he chuckled and his shrewd old face fell into countless creases as he could not contain his amusement. Sherlock Holmes pushed the photograph of Jesse James back towards Burton King, "Study the hand which grips the Colt butt and tell me what occurs to you."

King studied the picture. "He had a large hand, with long thick fingers, just as does Al Jennings."

The detective passed his lens to the director, "How many fingers do you see?"

"Well, I'll be gosh darned, Jesse was missing his third finger!" gasped King.

"Exactly, study again the very clear modern pictures of Jennings and I think you will agree that he has his full complement of digits. But, if any doubt lingers, a personal interview with Jennings will completely resolve the doubt. I think I can safely say that Al Jennings is *not* Jesse James. Of course, he could be related to him, or at least be a close compatriot, someone who was a member of the notorious James gang, known by reputation even to a simple British subject. This would account for his knowledge of James's background."

I can hardly say that King's reaction was that of a delighted man. He growled, "Darn it, as Jesse James he was worth a fortune to the studio and himself, but as Al Jennings he is just a bit part actor who might only get a job on the movie as an advisor for fifty bucks a week!"

"Then let it remain our secret, Mr King, and let us hope that others will miss this rather obvious detail."

King looked relieved, "You are a straight shooter, Mr Holmes, we'll get him fixed up with a special glove or something. Why, Winkle has three fingers missing but nobody ever notices it."

"Winkle?" I asked.

"Sure, you know, Harold Lloyd!"

We were introduced to a number of personalities at the studio: actors, technicians and scene shifters. All seemed to have a common respect for Houdini as a performer but it seemed to me from their responses to Holmes's questions that very few had actually liked him. Yet it seemed to me that none of them would have actually wished him harm, let alone death.

Later that day Beatrice Houdini took us, at Holmes's request, to the workshop and storehouse where once all of the Houdini properties had been built and housed when not in active use. Gone now were the Chinese Water Torture Cell and the vast cabinet that had accommodated the famous Vanishing Elephant and all the other main attractions that had made Houdini a household name. There remained only a few smaller properties, crates of books, paper (the term which we learned meant posters and other publicity material) and two rather downtrodden-looking middle-aged men who were still retained to oversee the demise of the Houdini theatrical empire. They were both called Jim, Vickery and Collins respectively. Bess addressed both as Jim, but only one of them would respond when the name was called. It was all in the tone of voice: a shrill, insistent calling for Mr Vickery and a rather more gentle but none the less demanding tone for Mr Collins.

Whilst Bessie was in a small partitioned-off section, attending to some bills and invoices, Holmes questioned the two men who had been Houdini's right and left hands. "I suppose Houdini was an exacting and demanding employer?"

"Yes and no, we knew his business inside out, on and off stage. He knew he could trust us so we didn't get the rough edge of his tongue as much as some," replied Vickery, to which Collins added, "It was the new or temporary assistants who got all that. He had to be strict, after all in an emergency they had to do what they were told and not argue. Sometimes his life would depend on it."

Holmes touched upon the incident of the broken ankle which Hardeen had mentioned. They both looked rather shamefaced. Vickery said, "My fault, I hired this Hunky who said he had once worked for De Kolta. I thought he knew his business, but . . . "

"I don't see why you should blame yourself Jim, the guy was shown exactly what to do, he seemed intelligent, how were you to know that he would jerk the rope like that," said Collins, "could have killed the guv'nor, Mr Holmes, because he needed all his health and strength to get out of that water torture cell."

"I believe his name was Zoltan.

Was that his Christian name?" asked Holmes.

"Nah, he was called George, with an s on the end of it."

Between us Holmes and I drew them out concerning Georges Zoltan. Beyond the fact that he appeared to be of Hungarian ancestry, we learned that he was tall, blue eyed and had a shock of blond hair. Collins said, "Usually the guv'nor was not keen on tall helpers for obvious reasons but there are times when you can't get all the help you need."

"He always wore a kind of gold cross on a chain around his neck, we had to tell him to tuck it inside his shirt when he appeared before an audience. It was unusual, the cross had a kind of snake curled around it," added Vickery.

Neither man could think of anything else of significance that had occurred during the countdown to Houdini's dramatic demise. They confirmed all that Bess had related concerning the incident in the dressing room that had led up to that fatal punch in the abdomen. When they were asked if the Hungarian had been present they said that he had been dismissed very shortly after the incident of Houdini's broken ankle.

Eventually we were joined again by Daisy and Bess, who carried a deed box from the enclosed section. "This is the famous box that is not supposed to be opened until 1976 but I think you should open it Mr Detective and start detecting! If there is something in there to give a clue to foul play, I feel that ignoring his request is justified."

★ ★ ★

That evening back at the hotel, Holmes placed the deed box upon one of the beds and then threw himself into an easy chair and began attending to his pipe. Far from his normal environment, he was forced to charge it with tobacco from a simple pouch, like any normal being — the Turkish slipper being some three thousand miles away. He was in no hurry to open the box, a fact which began to irritate me after half-an-hour or so. I admit that I was anxious to know if anything lay within which might give some clue to the bizarre circumstances surrounding Houdini's death. The box boasted no lock but was bound with cord and the knots were sealed with red wax. After what seemed an age, Holmes arose from his chair, took out his pocket knife and cut the cords. He threw the lid open and we both peered into the box. There were a few artifacts and keepsakes within, including small framed photographs of Bess and a small white terrier dog. A folder proved to be filled with neatly drawn plans and diagrams with numerous pencilled captions on their borders. On the folder cover itself was written, "To be delivered to Mr Walter B Gibson should he be still in the land of the living. If he has passed on, please give it to the editor of the leading American magicians' magazine for publication."

Holmes grunted. "Professional secrets, doubtless pertaining to great illusions not yet produced. I must consult Walter Gibson, of course. Naturally I cannot hand him the folder, he must wait until January 1976. Necessity has made us break some ethical rules but that does not mean that we can ride roughshod over Houdini's wishes and instructions."

"Is there anything else in the box?" I enquired.

Holmes explored its depths. "There is one more interesting item and a few papers." His hand reappeared, holding delicately what appeared to be a gold chain to which a small gold cross was attached. He placed it carefully upon a bed pillow that we might examine it. The links of the chain were extremely small and the cross no more than an inch high. There was no clasp so obviously the chain loop was intended to be placed over the head. One link was broken, so that the cross had attached to it two separate lengths of chain; one about eighteen inches long and the other perhaps six inches or so. Holmes took his lens to it and studied it most carefully before he spoke.

"It is of Balkan gold, less valuable than that most usually employed. None the less, the links would be of great strength and to break one would require considerable force." He lifted the chain by its broken link and studied that particular unit carefully.

"Has it been cut do you think?" I asked.

"No, Watson, there is no clean break which would have been left by pliers or a jeweller's saw. This has been broken quite deliberately by sheer force, probably through it being deliberately torn from the neck of its wearer. A chain may be only as strong as its weakest link but even this, the weakest link, would have presented considerable resistance. The wearer would have been left with a very

171

nasty cut or gash on the left hand side of his neck."

"How can you know which side of the neck the chain would have damaged?"

He passed the lens to me and suggested that I examine the links at the end of the longer length of chain. To my surprise I detected what I could see to be blood stains. "By jove, Holmes, you are right and the struggle for the chain must have been quite prolonged for the blood from such a gash to be deposited on the chain.

Holmes next turned his attention to the cross itself, saying, "A crucifix, but with a difference. You see it has the representation of a snake entwined around it and there is a letter M etched into the very intersection of the cross."

I made a wild guess, "Could this stand for Mary, the blessed Virgin?"

Holmes shook his head. "No, my guess — and I am not given to guessing so I could be proved wrong — is that it stands for the word Magyar, given the Balkan gold and Houdini's Hungarian background."

"Surely if this belonged to Houdini it would take a different form. The Star of David perhaps, given his Jewish faith?"

"Exactly, but it is not Houdini's, although possibly it was he who tore it from the neck of its wearer."

"Ah, but who?" I pondered.

Holmes threw me an admonishing glance. "Really, Watson you have allowed your grey matter to deteriorate through general lack of use during recent years. I believe it was Mr Jim Vickery who told us of one Georges Zoltan, of Hungarian extraction, hired as an assistant to Houdini but dismissed through causing a careless accident which fractured Houdinis ankle. He, or was it his colleague, who told us that Zoltan wore a cross with entwined snake around his neck?"

I had to admit that my memory

and observation had been dulled by lack of use. I changed the direction of the conversation. "What sort of a religious group do you think the cross represents?"

"At first I was tempted to think of international freemasonry. But, on reflection, I am more inclined to favour the idea that it is the emblem of a secret society. Perhaps an organization of extreme Magyar Nationalists?"

Sherlock Holmes took a pad from his pocket and a gold propelling pencil. He laid the cross with its chain carefully back on the pillow and began to sketch it with quick deft strokes. The resulting drawing, whilst it would have found no place in the Royal Academy, was very clear in its observation of detail. Then having returned the pad and pencil to their various pockets he lifted the cross and returned it to the box.

"Houdini is trying to tell us something, Watson," he said, "but this is complicated by the fact that he is expecting to pass his message to the world of fifty years ahead. He may therefore reveal facts that could prove embarrassing to Mrs Houdini. We must tread carefully, my dear fellow, we must tread carefully."

This Pandora's Box of Houdini's yielded up to us a final item, which in turn yielded several others, for it was a small portfolio of letters. Holmes pointed to the tape which secured it, saying, "Tied by Houdini in person Watson, for did you ever see knots like those before?"

I admitted that I had not, even when tied by mariners. Holmes, after some thought, brought forth his pad and pencil again and, turning the page, sketched the knots.

When I enquired after his purpose he said, "Remember, Watson, I have to tie them again exactly as they are, so that they will present the same effect on their discoverers in 1976 as they have had upon us."

Only after he was completely happy with the sketch and considered that he could duplicate the knots, did Holmes untie the portfolio. The first item taken out was a letter typed upon an eight-by-ten-inch sheet of buff-tinted paper, bearing a head and shoulders likeness of Houdini in its left top corner. It read as follows:

Alhambra Theatre, Paris, France,
November 22nd 1913

My dear brother Dash,

Received your letter from Boston; you certainly have worked there often enough. Save your money and then you will not care if you go back there or not.

This is my new letterhead and it is not with gladness that I ordered same. The St Paul Printing Co so I hear 'indirectly' are selling your D C to handcuff experts. But I can't blame them for you have not offered to purchase what they have and I suppose they work on such a small margin that they must have their money.

Re the birthdays, I shall celebrate mine (?) always April 6th. It hurts me to think I can't talk it over with Darling Mother and as she always wrote me on April 6th that will be my adopted birth date.

Dash it's tough and I can't seem to get over it. Sometimes I feel all right but when a calm moment arrives I am as bad as ever. Time heals all wounds but a long time will have to pass before it will heal the terrible blow which mother tried to save me from knowing. But to other things or else I can't finish this letter. Am working on a few new things in illusion line and as soon as I accomplish anything will let you know. Have had a wonderful month, business however is dropping off. But am not worrying.

Hope all is well with you and your family, Bess joins me in sending love. Bess has not been well of late, can't understand it. Maybe she is sick? Do you remember that story? I shall never forget it.

Let me hear from you whenever convenient.

As ever your brother
Ehrich (Harry Houdini)

Address me in future care of Day's Agency as I shall spend December in London and all my work is in England until we return to America.

"What do you make of it Watson?" Typical of Holmes that he volunteered nothing, expecting me to put my poor lame military foot straight into the deep end.

"I think from our experience of the late Harry Houdini that he dictated it to a secretary for it is neatly typed and the grammar is reasonable, for an American. It is an old letter, dated all but a year before the outbreak of the Great War, moreover it was sent from Houdini to Hardeen. As it is the original and not a carbon copy one wonders why Houdini regained it and placed it among these mementoes, meant to be read in 1976? Oh yes and I wonder what D C means, in relation to Hardeen and the St Paul Printing Company?"

Holmes who had been nodding wisely at my comments, broke in, "The initials I would imagine refer to a die cut which the printers had evidently made expressly for Hardeen but for which they had not received payment. They may have sold it to a collector of such things or even to a rival. But the reference to 6 April as an *adopted* birth date interests me more."

Holmes, as he spoke to me, was rapidly writing a copy of the letter into his pocket pad with enormous speed in a shorthand of his own invention.

"Then the comments concerning his mother who, by our previous information, had died not long before the date of the letter. He expresses the natural grief of the bereaved, yet there seems to be the hint of more than this. One wonders what was this terrible blow which he says that his mother tried to shield him from? Also the reference to Bess and his question as to if she really is sick? Maybe Mrs Houdini is a hypochondriac?"

I did not have the answers to his questions, but pondered them suitably. He finished writing and extracted another paper from the portfolio. This one was also typed and on eight-by-ten paper but with no date:

Apartment 63,
24 Morningside Drive,
New York City.

Dear Bess,

You must remember how our blessed mother would swell with pride when she displayed the worn prayer rug, don't you? I can still hear her boast in her gentle manner that the Kaiserin Josephine had walked on it many times when she visited some orphan asylum directly opposite our home. On these occasions her royal highness looked in on our family to pay respect to our important and intellectual dad. However, the rug was associated with a tragic episode. There was an infant son, Ehrich, of our household at that time.

This babe, through a fall, died suddenly and broke the hearts of both our parents. Both of them said, if ever another son were to be their blessing his name would be Ehrich. You know Bess, in Jewish families, newborn children are named for the departed. Later, when the family was settled in Appleton, Wisconsin, another son came to bless the home and this child was Ehrich. I am sure you have heard mother tell you all this before.

Fondest thoughts to you and your dear family. Greetings to Dr Saint.

from Gladys.

Again Holmes spoke as he wrote but this time spared me expressing my deductions. "This letter is even more interesting Watson; evidently it was sent to Mrs Houdini by her husband's sister, Gladys. The mother she refers to is obviously her own and Houdini's. She displays a likeness for social climbing — note the references to the Kaiserin Josephine and her intellectual and important father. The letter tells me that this lady is writing to Beatrice Houdini by arrangement so to speak. She tells her those things which, as a member of the Weiss family, even if only by marriage, she must have heard a thousand times. It is as if Beatrice said to her, 'Gladys, I want you to write to me to this or that effect, that I may show the letter to . . . '"

I perused the letter again and I took

his point. "Maybe, I said, it was for the benefit of the insurance companies?"

I had to agree that the letter had a false ring to it, for one written by a sister-in-law. Holmes nodded. "That is possible Watson, for it makes stress upon Houdini's birth being in Appleton, Wisconsin, which has always been claimed by everyone we have spoken to and in all published details about Houdini's life and career that has come our way. The suggestion regarding the birth of an earlier infant Ehrich, and Houdini being named after his late baby brother does not ring true. I know something of Jewish customs and have never heard of such a practice. This encourages me to believe that Houdini was in fact born in Hungary but wished the world to believe him an American by birth. This is rather borne out by the reference in the letter from Houdini to Hardeen regarding the question surrounding his actual birth date."

I was beginning to understand what

was in Holmes's mind. "If Houdini had stated 6 April 1874, Appleton, Wisconsin, as his date and place of birth on his insurance documents and these details were later proved to be incorrect, might this not affect the settlements to Beatrice Houdini?"

"Exactly, Watson, and this is why the good lady has never mentioned these details to us, other than that his published biographies are correct. She hopes to let that particular sleeping dog lie. Yet she is keen that I should find reason to suppose that her husband died through foul play, in order to benefit from this further policy. We must tread carefully, Watson, and only reveal to the world that which we have been engaged to investigate. Mind you, I intend to know all other pertinent facts connected with the matter, for my own satisfaction."

Obviously something of an ethical dilemma might eventually present itself to us. But we agreed to continue with our enquiries until more substantial facts presented themselves before making any decisions of a definite nature. The portfolio had not yet yielded all of its treasures and another piece of paper was extracted and examined. This was a smaller sheet and it was badly typed and greatly misspelled, as follows:

Chapter one
by Theodore Hardeen.

Father insulted by prince Ehrich challenged to a dule which was fought following morning and father killing his opponent. Then fled to London and stayed there for a time after which he took sailing vessel to New York.

After reaching New York kept going to Appleton Wisconsin, where he had friends by the name of Hammel, one being Mayor of Appleton at that time — about 1874. A short time passed and as there were no synagogues in the town the Mayor wanted to send to

Milwaukee for one, but up spoke Mr S M Weiss and said "why I am a Rabbi!" and was given the job. He at once sent for Mrs W and soon after her arrival Houdini was born April 6th 1874. And he was named Ehrich Prach after Prince Ehrich.

After carefully reading and examining this item, Holmes said, "Upon my word Watson, friend Hardeen is even more original with his spelling than is his sister. Moreover, he is not used to typing for he often strikes the wrong keys. Again it smacks of an almost pathetic attempt to justify Houdini's claimed American birth and date. Like the other documents it has been placed here with the intention of justifying the subject's background claims."

"Why do you think it states Chapter One as its heading, when there are scarcely more than a dozen lines?"

"I imagine it is the first sheet from an intended Houdini biography, possibly given to Houdini for his approval," Holmes replied.

Through a close study of his own drawings Holmes was able to duplicate faithfully the tying of the portfolio, which he returned to the famous box. I decided to take a bath at this point and was absent from the bedroom for perhaps a quarter of an hour. When I returned, slightly to my surprise I observed that Houdini's secret box had been re-tied and sealed in such a manner that it would have been all but impossible to see any difference from its original appearance. Only a scientific examination would have revealed that it had ever been opened.

"You see, Watson, the secret box can now be safely returned to Mrs Houdini. When next it is opened neither you nor I, or the good lady herself, are likely to be interrogated concerning its history save by means of a spirit seance."

★ ★ ★

I telephoned Beatrice Houdini concerning the safe return of the box and she arranged to send Jim Vickery to fetch it, having first enquired if Holmes had discovered anything pertinent within it. I told her, quite truthfully, that I thought he had found some interesting documents which might or might not advance his investigations. She suggested that we call upon her on the morrow, which I agreed to on Holmes's behalf as well as for myself. Her voice upon the telephone was rather more staccato than when she spoke in person.

Within the hour Jim Vickery presented himself to collect the box. He expressed his satisfaction at its unaltered appearance. "Gentlemen, I know that you will not intimate to a living soul that the box has been opened. I promised the guv'nor that it would remain as it was for fifty years but when Mrs Houdini confided in me the reason for your enquiries, I had to admit that breaking my word might have been justified. Even Jim Collins knows nothing of the true reason for your involvement. If there was foul play and who knows there might have been, then I sure hope that you can prove it for the sake of Mrs Houdini. I believe that extra policy is for a tidy few bucks. Oh by the way, Walter Gibson is going to call round at seven. He would like to talk with you, take you to dinner, something like that. Wally is a nice guy but he doesn't know too much, except about Houdini's magical secrets and escape methods. I wouldn't tell him too much either — remember, he is a writer."

Holmes thanked Vickery for the information and suggestion. "It is good to know of your devotion to Mrs Houdini, sir, and I will bear in mind what you have told me."

Promptly at seven a bellboy knocked at our door and announced that there was a visitor awaiting us in the lobby. The boy presented Holmes with a visiting card which proclaimed that

Walter B Gibson was an author and journalist. Holmes gave the boy a dime. "Tell Mr Gibson we will be with him directly — and thank you, Billy."

The bellboy started, not at the magnitude of the tip but at the use of that Christian name. "Say, mister, how did youz know my monicker?"

Holmes smiled. "It was a reflex, I once employed a page boy with that name."

I chuckled, remembering the passing parade of twelve-year-olds who had been 'Billy' in their turn at 221b Baker Street. Such substitutions had never been noticed by the most observant man in Great Britain.

Gibson turned out to be a well built, tall, young man with a luxuriant head of light brown hair. He was dressed neatly — but not formally — in a hound's-tooth check jacket with the currently fashionably close-fitting trousers of a contrasting hue. He greeted us both heartily and spoke with the all but British tones of a

New Englander. "Mr Holmes, Doctor Watson, I am so happy to meet you both."

I estimated his age to be perhaps thirty but he was older than that in his mannered composure. He suggested that we join him for dinner, an invitation that we were glad to accept.

We were transported in his impressive Daimler to a restaurant in an area which he referred to as Little Italy, where we were soon dealing with large portions of spaghetti and meat sauce. I had some difficulty at first in dealing with the long, unfamiliar strands of pasta, until I took my cue from Holmes who, ignoring the knife, wound the spaghetti deftly into a spoon with his fork.

Gibson was delighted. "I see you are familiar with the only way to deal with the stuff Mr Holmes!"

"I have travelled in Italy, but Watson is more used to the roast beef at Simpsons. Your country is a young and lively one, Mr Gibson, but you are all but mindful of our fellow countrymen."

"Well, I have resided long in New England, which you must explore whilst you are here. You know there are fields, meadows, lanes and farms in Connecticut that would make you swear you were back at home." He went on to tell us a little about himself. "I am a writer by trade but have dabbled in the magical side of show business. I even ran a magic shop in Philadelphia briefly, two or three years back, but demonstrating card tricks and sucker die boxes was not my idea for a career. Of course everything we do in this life has its purpose, if we can take advantage of it. It was through the magic-shop episode that I met Dunninger and later Houdini. They were both able to employ my journalistic skills and Houdini put me onto a job ghostwriting a book of magic for Howard Thurston, perhaps the greatest living magician but no author. Tell me, what is your own special interest in Houdini, Mr Holmes?"

There was only the shortest of pauses. "My friend and colleague Doctor Watson has been requested by the editor of *The Strand* magazine to write a series of articles on Houdini. Since my retirement from active professional life he has been hard put to provide Sir Arthur Conan Doyle with material for episodes from my activities. He has decided to branch out as a writer rather than a provider of research. He has gained all the sap possible from this dry old stick and now seeks other avenues for journalistic exploration."

I took up the theme, quite surprising myself with my ingenuity. "That is right Mr Gibson and having read all that has been published concerning Houdini's life and career, I felt I must seek new or rather hitherto unknown facts about that enigmatic man. Holmes, ever supportive, agreed to accompany me here. After all, his celebrity may well open doors to me that would remain closed to a mere medic and scribbler."

Gibson was vaguely dismissive of my words. "Oh come, Doctor, I know that those diaries of yours must have been well written as well as accurate to enable Conan Doyle to produce such wonderful exploits and adventures. Indirectly you can be said to have invented the modern detective story; something for which I will be forever grateful to you. I am also, in my small way, a writer of mystery and detective fiction. I have had quite a few things published in the field which we call pulp. Literally it means that they are printed on paper rescued from the salvage yards and pulped. This enables the publishers to produce quite good books and magazines at highly competitive prices. But I'm trying to break into radio. It is the coming field for writers — you should investigate this field yourself, Doctor. I have an idea for a character which I call 'the Shadow'. He is a mystery figure who observes and narrates amazing stories; just the thing for radio. But what can

I tell you about Harry that will help you?"

I did some quick thinking and began to ask the sort of questions which I thought might bring forth answers to assist Holmes, yet was careful to ask other questions so that Gibson might not put two and two together. After all, I had already decided that he was more than a shrewd man with great imagination. "Is the generally accepted account of Harry Houdini's first meeting with his wife accurate?" I began.

"Well, hardly," he said, "you mean the story that Harry was hired as an entertainer at a party that she attended and spilled some coloured water from one of his tricks down the front of her dress?"

"That's right, I have read that he got his mother to make a new dress and took it round to this big house where she lived with her parents, who were Catholics."

Gibson laughed. "Well, certainly Mr

and Mrs Rahner were Catholics, but Bessie was no debutante, as implied. No, she and another girl were working at some dive in the Bowery as the Rahner Sisters — a song and dance act — when Harry met her first."

"Did not her parents object to their association on religious grounds?" I continued.

"Not nearly as much as Cecelia did, that's Harry's mother. She nearly went berserk when she heard that her good Jewish son planned to marry a shiksa!" He answered my puzzled look by saying, "That's a Yiddish term of disrespect for a Christian girl."

Many were the questions that I asked, occasionally slipping in one that I knew Holmes would have wanted. "He was born, was he not, in Appleton, Wisconsin?"

Gibson answered in a hesitant and guarded fashion. "Yes, on 6 April 1874. If you have heard any differently, Doctor, you are on the wrong track."

Quickly, I asked another bland

question, "Will you write anything about Houdini yourself Mr Gibson?"

He relaxed. "Oh yes, Harry has left me a fund of magical secrets, some that he used and many new items. A couple of years ago he gave me this material bidding me to publish it after his death. Bear in mind that he was all but twenty-five years my senior. He suggested that I meted it out in a series of books to be published at measured intervals throughout my own lifetime. He explained that this would not only be good for my own writing career but would keep his name alive. Alas, I had expected to start work on the first volume in perhaps twenty or even thirty years' time. I little guessed that the first volume would become possible so soon."

I asked yet another bland question before daring to enquire, "What did you make of the events leading to Houdini's death?"

Gibson's reply this time had not the guarded style of his response to my enquiry about Houdini's birth date. "Nothing sinister there, Doctor. The student who punched him in the guts was without guile. Harry was preoccupied when he was asked if this could be done. As for the peritonitis that followed, well . . . I don't need to tell you, Doctor, that an immediate operation would probably have restored him to health. It is only because he neglected it with this ridiculous the-show-must-go-on obsession that you are prevented from having this conversation with Houdini himself. I believe you both met him a few years back?"

Holmes decided to answer this question. "Yes, he came to me for advice concerning his suspicions about a spiritualistic medium, or rather one purporting to be such. Sir Arthur Conan Doyle was in danger of being deceived and Houdini wished to expose the fraud."

"Marina and her husband, Doctor Blackthorne? They needed to be exposed," Gibson nodded wisely.

"Marina's so-called spirit voice made a few threats," Gibson chuckled. "Oh sure, I wish I had a dollar for every time Harry called guides! Just sour grapes, believe me."

Later, after Walter Gibson had driven us back to the Brownstone and taken his leave, we sat in the hotel lounge and talked over coffee and liqueurs. I said to Holmes, rather warmly, "My dear fellow, you might have warned me as to what you planned to say by way of explaining our interest in Houdini!"

Holmes smiled, almost kindly. "But, my dear Watson, you responded splendidly to my suggestion just as I knew you would. Tell me what did you make of friend Gibson?"

"I liked him, he had a very honest, friendly and helpful manner. Though I did notice a rather sharp response to the questions concerning Houdini's place and date of birth."

"Yes, I noted this too. I suspect that his loyalty to Houdini made him respond as he did; possibly knowing of some doubt regarding these generally accepted facts. I think his response, added to suggestions made in the letters from the portfolio, make Houdini's place and date of birth somewhat suspect. Of course, I realize that it is not part of my terms of reference to investigate such things, save if they have some bearing on this matter. So I think that we will not mention these particular suspicions to Mrs Houdini for the present."

Nor did we do so, in fact, when we saw Beatrice Houdini on the following day. We were at her home by invitation partaking of refreshment when she asked, "Say what do you make of Wally Gibson?"

"A charming young man, who tried to be helpful to us," I responded.

"He does not seem to subscribe to the suspicions of foul play which are our main concern," Holmes added.

"What about that secret box? I have not opened it as you will have seen and say you did a good job on making it look as if you had not!"

"Better that it stays just as it is until the official year of revelation," Holmes said. "My dear Mrs Houdini, there is nothing in the box save magicians' secrets and a few personal artefacts."

He gave her a resumé of the letters that we had found, but laid no stress upon our suspicions regarding the birth details. He also mentioned the chain and cross.

"Ah, that will be some magical award I guess, he was always being given medals and such. I got a case full of them some place. But I can't think why Gladys's letter to me should have got in there," Bess said when Holmes described the cross and its design she became impatient. It was obvious to me that it rang no bells in her memory.

"You know what you guys want to be doing is questioning them doctors and students," she said, "you might learn something there. You know I'm anxious to get this thing cleared up and get that nice cheque from the Acme

201

Insurance Company:"

To my surprise Holmes said, "Dear lady, my thoughts entirely and I will be leaving for Montreal on the morrow."

This news placated her. "Well, that's more like it. You going too, Doc?"

Before I could splutter some non-committal reply Holmes said, "Doctor Watson will indeed accompany me as his medical knowledge will be most helpful."

Later he was to tell me that far from accompanying him I was to go to Appleton, Wisconsin, to consult the birth registration.

On the morning that followed we both took the train, though in different directions. Holmes's journey, from New York to Montreal, was of an uncomplicated nature, whilst mine required a change at Chicago, itself a distance of some seven hundred rail miles from New York. I will, dear reader, relate my own experiences before repeating the account of the adventures which Holmes was to relate to me upon my return.

First let me give you my general feelings concerning the American railways. I regard the trains and service as absolutely superb. Moreover I really do enjoy those special features, the club and observation cars. Regarding the latter, it is a rather uncanny feeling to stand there on the platform and watch the scenery disappear as if before you have even seen it. Quite a different sensation from travelling in such a manner that you can see straight ahead of you. As for the club car, why how very pleasant it is to sit as if in a rather informal restaurant and be able to talk with your fellow passengers over a smoke and a cup of coffee. I suppose the day will come when aviation will replace the great steam-bellowing monsters of the American railway. I feel sure that travel by aeroplane will never be quite as pleasant.

The atmosphere of the train makes conversation possible with interesting, amusing and sometimes even quite bizarre persons. I encountered a gentleman, dressed in a rather loud check suit and a black bowler hat who told me that he was leaving New York and bound for Chicago on account of his health. He further explained that "New York is getting too hot for me, see?"

When I enquired as to the climate in Chicago he said that there would be no problems as, "Big Al will see to that!"

When I enquired as to his occupation he said that he was a collector, for Big Al, so I asked if this gentleman dealt in antiquities?

"New money, old money, it's all the same!" he told me. I assumed that his employer collected bank notes old and new, an interesting hobby.

"Say what's your racket, buddy?" he wanted to know.

I told him that I was a medical man and he asked, "Say, do you know Doc Brady? If ever you get a slug in ya, Doc

Brady will attend to it and no questions asked!" He rolled up his trouser leg and displayed a healed bullet wound.

I examined it with professional interest and remarked, "The stitching is splendid. Tell me, was it a hunting accident?"

He laughed and touched his nose in a very strange gesture. "Oh sure, Doc, Big Al sent me out hunting and I had a slight accident, haw, haw!"

When the train reached Chicago, after a great many hours which had seemed to pass very quickly, we both descended from the train and he shook hands with me, wishing me good luck. He also handed me a piece of card. "Any time anyone gives you a hard time, Doc, show 'em this. It's a spare, I got my own."

Then he was away in a taxi leaving me to gaze at a small piece of pasteboard upon which was printed: THE BEARER IS A FRIEND OF AL CAPONE. DON'T GIVE HIM A HARD TIME!

From Chicago I took another train to

Appleton, Wisconsin, which was only about a hundred and fifty miles (a short journey indeed in comparison to that which I had already made). I put up at a small timber-built hotel called the Splendide, pleasantly sited quite near to Lake Winnebago.

I will not tire the reader with accounts of my exploration of Appleton. Enough to say that it was a pleasant enough small American town. I found the registrar's office fairly easily, where I discovered that there was a record volume from 1880 which should, according to the lady assistant who was most helpful, contain the information I was seeking. I soon discovered the Weiss family entries. The record of the birth of Theodore Weiss, 29 February 1876 showed me that I had the correct family. But there was no mention of the birth of an Ehrich Weiss. Examination of census records, however, did mention all the family including Samuel, Cecelia, Nathan, Leopold, Gladys and Ehrich.

I probably made quite a nuisance of myself at the record office but I had to be sure that there was no mistake. The kind lady did say that the records from before 1880 were a trifle sketchy but that no other notation was likely to exist. I returned to New York, convinced that Ehrich Weiss (Harry Houdini) had *not* been born in Appleton, Wisconsin, although he had definitely resided there as a child.

As Holmes had not arrived back from Montreal, I spent an evening at the theatre. I had not intended this but, whilst taking a stroll near the hotel I encountered a façade that proclaimed BURLESQUE. On an impulse I entered the theatre having ever been fond of satire. But I tell you, dear reader, I have no idea to this day as to just what was being burlesqued! The performance was of a very dubious nature, consisting mainly of young women very lightly clothed. After about ninety minutes, I decided that it was not the sort of thing that I could sit through.

The next day Mrs Houdini took her companion Daisy and myself to the opera and later to dinner. When she asked where I had been I told her Chicago, which was indeed true. She asked the reason for my visit to what she called the Windy City. I told her that I had relatives there, which was not a complete untruth as I believe a distant cousin of mine did once settle in Chicago. When asked for the name of my relatives I said (searching my memory for a convenient name and remembering the card that the strange man on the train had given me), "Al Capone."

Mrs Houdini looked at me very strangely and then stuck her elbow into my ribs and dropped one of her eyelids. As I endeavoured to straighten my jacket the programme from the burlesque play fell to the ground. Both ladies had eyes like saucers as Bess handed it back to me, saying, "Don't worry, honey, I won't snitch to your pal!"

Three more days were to pass before I heard anything from Holmes, and the museums and Central Park Zoo were beginning to pall by the time his wire arrived.

DR JOHN WATSON BROWNSTONE HOTEL NEW YORK CITY STOP ARRIVING GRAND CENTRAL STATION SEVEN PM FRIDAY STOP MY INVESTI-GATIONS HAVE PROVED FRUITFUL STOP PLEASE SEARCH FOR SOME SCOTTISH SHAG AS I HAVE BEEN UNABLE TO OBTAIN IT STOP REGARDS SHERLOCK HOLMES

As ever, Holmes was quite unable to observe a brevity when sending a telegram. I was glad to hear that his expedition had been more valuable than my own, but I certainly did not look forward to searching New York tobacconists for his favourite Scottish Mixture. However, I was indeed able to find some, though I had to go all the way to the East Side to get it. It was sold in unfamiliar packages rather than weighed out as it was at home. These packages bore a trademark design depicting a Scot with beard and a checked tam-o'-shanter, dressed in tartans.

I duly presented myself at the Grand Central Station and met the nearest scheduled incoming train from Montreal but Holmes did not emerge at the barrier with the arriving people. Just as I was about to depart to the refreshment room to await the arrival of another train from Montreal, a tap on my shoulder proclaimed the presence of Sherlock Holmes.

"My dear Watson, you are looking well. New York suits your constitution. The heat does not bother you after your experience of Afghanistan." He explained that his investigations had taken him from Montreal to Detroit.

"You might have let me know which train to meet!" I said rather warmly.

"Oh come old fellow, I knew where to find you and one has to watch the number of words used in a wire."

From a man who had not hesitated to use fourteen words concerning his tobacco I found this ludicrous but said no more about it. Holmes looked bronzed and fit, dressed in his alpaca jacket and carrying his elderly Gladstone bag. He was smoking a cigar, about which he remarked, "These Prince Georges are extremely reasonable, as they should be. I took one apart and discovered that it was made from the leaves of a cabbage plant, sweetened with molasses but, strangely, extremely pleasant to smoke. Did you get me the Scottish Mixture?"

When I nodded my assent he was delighted, saying. "I could find none either in Montreal or Detroit but I'm sorry to have put you to the trouble of going all the way to the East Side to get it!"

Although I knew his methods so well,

I had no conception as to how he knew this fact and I said so.

"My dear Watson you have some hairs from a capuchin monkey still upon your jacket. The organ grinders of the East Side, usually of Italian extraction, use these animals to help them beg for small coinage. These itinerants are excluded from our side of the city by law therefore the presence of these traces, plus the knowledge of your errand, told their own story."

"How can you be sure that the monkey was a capuchin? I have no idea as to its particular type. All I know is that the wretched thing was ordered to jump upon my shoulder in its quest for nickels and dimes!"

"Well, apart from the fact that the greater number of these animals are of that breed, due to their placid disposition and ease of purchase in the United States, I recognized the texture of the hairs."

For the first time in many years a shadow of doubt concerning one of

Holmes's deductions had cast itself upon my mind. But he dispelled it at once. "There are eight hundred and forty-two different simian species upon this planet. I once prepared a monograph upon them and the detection of their species through an examination of their hairs. The work included actual samples from each. The capuchin hair is easily remembered." He took a single example between his finger and thumb from my coat and held it up to the light. "Notice the dark brown colour graduating down to a pale tan towards the root."

I stalked off, slightly peeved, and the man who had once been the world's only consulting detective followed me, chuckling.

We repaired to the refreshment room where we sat up upon revolving stools at a long counter. A young girl with bobbed hair placed a glass of iced water before each of us and said something which I simply could not translate into English. Holmes appeared to understand, having a perfect ear for dialect. "Yes, I'll have two fried eggs, sunny-side up, with some ham and fried potatoes. I'll take a Java, black, and what would you like, Watson?" Really he had learned quite a bit more than I had about that strange deviation which is American English. I took some scrambled eggs and coffee with cream.

"Really, Holmes are you going to continue with small talk and keep me in ignorance of your findings?" I rounded on Holmes, at last. "By the way I had no luck whatsoever at the record office in Appleton. I could find no record of the birth of an Ehrich Weiss, although the census for 1880 did reveal the whole Weiss family as residents."

He nodded. "It was then just as I suspected but I am grateful to you, Watson, for your confirmation; I had to be sure." He pushed the remains of his meal away from him, muttering to the effect that American portions were wastefully liberal and then continued.

"As I of course knew before I set out, the McGill University is closed for the summer recess. But I did manage to contact quite a few people locally who study there, including the student who struck those blows in question. He convinced me of his own complete innocence of any sort of deliberate complicity but I feel sure from what he told me that he was the unwitting tool of another. He said that a Hungarian, who sounded from his description to be friend Georges Zoltan, was the one who told him of Houdini's ability to withstand heavy blows to the abdomen and more, even suggesting that he put this ability to the test. In fact, Zoltan even suggested that no warning should be given! As it happens, he ignored this latter piece of advice although, as we know, unfortunately it made no difference in the end.

"The manager of the Princess Theatre was helpful in telling me of a foreigner who was much in evidence in the vicinity during Houdini's occupancy of the theatre. He even caught the man in the act of trying to interfere with some of Houdini's properties backstage but he thought that he was a souvenir hunter and simply threw him out of the building. Although Vickery and Collins and the rest of the company did not see him, Zoltan was never far away during that week. Add all of this to the minor accidents earlier in the tour, culminating in the broken ankle which almost cost Houdini his life, and Zoltan's involvement, we can now be sure that he was intent upon causing Houdini great harm, trying first one and then another tactic, which must by trial and error eventually lead to serious injury, even death.

"Detroit, the next town of the tour and the place where Houdini died, was the next logical place to visit. Evidently, according to the staff of the Garrick Theatre, Detroit, Houdini and his company went straight there rather than to his hotel, as the baggage had been delayed. The manager said that Houdini actually helped to uncrate it despite being obviously in great pain. Evidently he was examined just before the opening performance by a Dr Leo Dretzka, who confirmed an acute appendicitis and demanded that he go straight to hospital. Friend Houdini ignored this advice and managed to get through that show, though in terrible pain and with great difficulty. During the interval he was further examined and found to have a temperature of 104. The manager said that he made light of this, quipping to the nurse, 'When it reaches 105 you want to sell!'

"After the final curtain he was rushed by ambulance to the Grace Hospital, where he was operated upon. His brothers, Theodore and Nathaniel, and his sister, Gladys, joined Bess at his bedside, according to Dr LeFevre, to whom I was able to speak. According to the doctor he made a good recovery under the circumstances, being soon in good spirits, if very weak but then, apparently a rather strange thing happened. A doctor, with a heavy foreign accent, arrived and removed Houdini to another private ward. From then on he got weaker and at about 1.30 on the morning of 31 October, he died. Bess was at his side and was quite hysterical when his body was removed by the new doctor and his team."

I waited for him to continue but he seemed to want to be sure that I understood all that he had said. I remarked, "I suppose you have just confirmed that which was already known or suspected regarding Zoltan's involvement, at least by ourselves, but this business of the appearance of a strange foreign doctor seems entirely new. You suggest that the removal of the body was rather hastily done. Surely Bess saw his body again before he was buried?"

"Well, there, Watson, is the strange thing. She didn't. She was told by Doctor Korda, which proved to be his name, that the nature of the illness and treatment had grossly disfigured Houdini's appearance soon after death, and with her own delicate health, it would be better for her to try to remember him as he had been."

I whistled. "That's a bit hard to swallow, Holmes. As a medical man I know of no reason for such sudden disfigurement after death from peritonitis."

"Nor I and I asked Dr LeFevre if he had questioned this but he said that his involvement had ceased with the appearance of Houdini's own specialist team, as he called them. To me and to you I'll be bound, the whole episode begins to be suspect. But wait Watson, there is more and the plot thickens."

There was another long and irritating pause whilst Holmes charged his pipe with some of the Scottish Mixture, which I'd had the foresight to bring. The acrid smoke caused distress to other patrons of the refreshment room and we were persuaded to leave. As we stood out on the concourse, Holmes continued his narration: "Houdini, Watson, had been experimenting with a trick coffin, a huge affair, of metal which would enable him to be buried alive for more than twelve hours before being exhumed. Believe it or not, he was actually buried in that coffin, which miraculously found its way to the hospital in a convenient manner. It had not been at the theatre with his other properties but was sent for from New York. The mysterious medical team and Dr Korda travelled with the coffin, on the train in the baggage car. The rest we know, for there was evidently a swift burial in accordance with the Jewish religion and he was laid to rest next to his mother at the Machpelah Cemetery in Brooklyn."

That night we reported to Bessie Houdini. I took my cue from Holmes as to just how much she was, at this stage, to be told or questioned upon. He did not, I noted, lay too much stress upon the strange events of the

Hungarian medical team's involvement. But she did volunteer the information that she did not see Harry again after he had died in her arms.

"The forty-eight hours that followed are lost in a mist of horror and alcohol! I admit that I was smashed most of the time. Theo and Nat held me up at the funeral and my unsteadiness was put down to grief and shock. So you really do suspect foul play, Sherlock. How soon can I contact the Acme Insurance Company? You know if it wasn't for all the insurance policies I wouldn't have a bean because Harry had lost most of his money in those dash blamed movies, and a lot of other people's too."

"I should be able to finalize everything within a month Mrs Houdini; there are a few investigations still to make," said Holmes.

"A month?" she almost shrieked, "I didn't expect it would take this long, don't you have what you need already?"

Holmes calmed her, although I did hear her muttering to Daisy about our 'eating their heads off at my expense . . . '

The morning that followed found us at the Hungarian Embassy where a request for an interview with the ambassador was compromised to provide one with an assistant. He took us to his office and indicated deep leather chairs where we might sit. His name was Gindl and he was as helpful as it was probably possible for him to be. No, he had no records of a Georges Zoltan or a Dr Korda as Hungarian nationals resident in the United States, and he could not provide the birth record of Ehrich Weiss which we required. He did tell us that if we were to go to Budapest we might consult the records there. "If that Hungarian national was born in Budapest his record, even from so long ago, will exist."

Holmes showed him the sketch of the cross and chain. He was rather startled. "It is the emblem of a reactionary organization, avowed to rid our new regime of all remnants of the monarchy. There was a fear at one time that some distant relative of the crown prince might still survive. There is another group of rather decadent royalists who have made some efforts at home rule and a revived monarchy in the Magyar Province."

Before we left the embassy, Holmes insisted that we inspect the portraits of the late royal family. There they were, Emperor Franz Joseph and all his relatives. The final portrait was of a well built man in a dress uniform. It was captioned, 'Ehrich Prach'.

Holmes decided to say nothing to Beatrice Houdini concerning our prospective journey to Budapest. He simply told her that he had to return to Great Britain to settle some business and domestic matters. This was true enough, we both had commitments to attend to. What he did not tell her was that we were planning to go to Hungary prior to returning to America.

Holmes promised that we would return as swiftly as we could.

The return to Britain was fairly uneventful and, once there, we speedily made arrangements required for another absence, thereafter taking the boat train to Paris from Victoria and travelling on to Hungary by a long and trying rail journey.

Part Three

The Magyar Connection

I HAD read something of the fate of Hungary during the aftermath of the Great War. I knew that the monarchy had been replaced, following the assassination of Franz Joseph, with a regime which promised to be of a democratic nature but which, as so often happens in such circumstances, turned out to be quite repressive. The great Austro-Hungarian Empire had been divided into numerous smaller states with results that would later prove a lack of wisdom.

We found Budapest to be a still great and lively capital, with café life and culture still strong yet with an underlying atmosphere of intrigue. As visiting foreigners we were regarded with great suspicion, followed more than once by strange furtive men, too obvious to be taken seriously as secret agents. Holmes indeed found them amusing and insisted on leaving little clues for them on café tables and then dropped ostentatiously into refuse boxes. These took the form of little sketches of the famous cross with serpent and of the union jack. From the main office of the registry of births and deaths we were directed to seek the registry at the Pest Jewish congregation at number twelve Sip Street, in that ghetto. A very different scene was presented by the Jewish quarter where the busy and serious-looking population contrasted strangely with the Hungarians of the city centre. Rows of neat but extremely basic little houses gave way to tenement blocks, from which emerged the tailors and goldsmiths who would have looked just as at home in parts of London's East End. None of the Tzigane influence here, rather an atmosphere of hard work and honesty. I had read often that a Hungarian would steal anything, yet in this Jewish quarter I felt safe and would have trusted any one of the people we encountered.

Twelve Sip Street proved to be a large and sombre building containing row upon row of dusty-looking, well bound but ageing volumes of records.

Holmes spoke to the assistant in German, as he had little Hungarian, and fortunately was understood. The correct volume was produced and for the payment of a tiny sum we were permitted to examine it. There, at last, was the elusive Ehrich Weiss, born to Samuel and Cecelia Weiss (née Steiner) on 24 March 1874. Holmes entered the exact wording of the document into his note pad.

As we made our way back to the city centre hotel where we were staying, Holmes remarked, "Well Watson, we have established beyond doubt the birth place and date of our late friend. It is rather as I suspected. His parents took him to the United States as a very young baby, possibly even smuggled him in and later claimed that he was born in Appleton. Evidently no one has ever thought to question this but I fear that Mrs Houdini might find her insurance with Acme null and void should this be revealed."

"Do you intend to make this fact known to them, or to anyone else?" I asked him.

He shook his head. "Come Watson, unless questioned upon this fact by some official authority we are not obliged to volunteer it. Our next quest is for the leaders of that organization which employed friend Zoltan and others; for there lies any chance of proving foul play concerning Houdini's death."

"Perhaps we have only to make ourselves known to those who rather obviously follow us about?"

Holmes smiled. "Oh no, Watson, the men you refer to are a little too obvious to be members of a secret society. My experience of that breed tells me that they would be far more — how can I put it — professional? No, the men in the trenchcoats are agents of the Hungarian government. They know not what they follow us for save that we are foreigners who ask a lot of questions. Those that we seek are of similar beliefs but they want to use a stronger iron fist than do the government."

When we returned to our hotel room, our need to speculate on when we would meet Zoltan's organization was quickly removed. Two men were in the room and one of them, who was sitting upon my bed, was holding a revolver as if actually in waiting for us, whilst the other looked up from a search of our luggage. The man with the gun grinned and said in English, "Please enter gentlemen, we want to have a little talk with you."

The man who was busying himself with our luggage put down Holmes's Gladstone and crossed to the door, closing and leaning back against it. The man on the bed gestured with his gun. "Be seated Mr Holmes, Doctor Watson, you are in no danger, yet."

Holmes and I sat upon the other bed and observed our captors. At length Holmes said, "What is it that you want from us, Mr Zoltan?"

The gunman started, but only very slightly. Then grinned broadly. "How do you know my name?"

"From the scar on your neck," replied Holmes, "in just the right position to have been caused by the gold chain when Houdini tore it from your neck."

I noticed that there was indeed a long scarcely healed scar on the left side of his neck.

Zoltan's smile melted slowly. "What else do you know?"

"Not a great deal, save that you caused several accidents to happen to Houdini, including the episode with the Montreal student which resulted in Houdini's death. I was hoping that you would be able to tell me why you wanted to kill him."

Zoltan smiled most menacingly. "No harm in telling you now, as you are not likely to leave Budapest alive. In fact, I doubt Mr Holmes if you or your busybody friend will even leave this hotel room. We are members of Magyar Straum, a society that believes that the new government, installed as League of Nations puppets, are not doing enough to clean the last of the aristocrats from the face of the earth."

Holmes made to take out his notebook but the gun was pushed into his chest. "Please take a small notebook from my inside jacket pocket, if you will not allow me to do so."

Zoltan patted Holmes' pockets then, reassured, signed for him to carry on. Holmes brought forth the book and turned to show the drawing of the cross. "This is your insignia is it not? Hardly a secret society, I think."

The man who was standing near the door spoke to Zoltan in Hungarian but Zoltan waved him to silence, "My friend wants to dispose of you now but I think you may know even more that could interest our leader. You and your friend will walk out of this hotel with us and you will use any acting ability you might have to make the four of us seem like the best of friends. One false move, one foolish word and we will blow your heads off."

Our feet were heavy as, with fixed smiles, we walked out of the hotel with our captors. They propelled us into a yard, rather like a huge roofless garage. Therein stood parked a huge lorry with an all-steel body. Aside from the driving cab the only entry to the vehicle was by means of two large rear doors which were secured by means of a solid bar, passing through an iron staple on each door. Immense iron padlocks were the means of security. It seemed obvious to me, that once inside the vehicle, there was no possible way out unless one's captors released the locks. Moreover, the inside of the van was lined entirely with zinc.

"By sheer coincidence this is the exact twin of the Siberian prison van from which Houdini actually escaped on his tour of Russia but unless you have the powers of the great Houdini — and I am sure you have not — you will not escape," said Zoltan. "Climb inside and you will be safe until we fetch our leader and take you to our headquarters. He is in a Mazurka bar round the corner, he doesn't like to get involved in the physical side of our activities." We were forced inside the vehicle at gun point, being told, "Shout all you want, once closed it will be quite soundproof."

My spirits reached an all-time low as the doors were slammed and we were locked inside the vehicle, unable even to see. I spoke quietly to Holmes, I don't know why, for there was no way that I could be heard save by him. "Holmes, do you think they really mean to kill us?"

"Probably," he said, "but I don't intend for us to hang around and find out."

He struck a vesta. His face and

form assumed eerie proportions by the flickering light of the match. He dropped to his knees and I could just make out that he was examining the inside base of the doors. He chuckled softly. I could not for one moment find anything to be amused by.

"We are not done yet, Watson. Would you believe it if I told you that among those details and plans in the secret box, destined eventually for Walter Gibson, was the secret of his escape from the Siberian prison van?"

I gasped. "And . . . and you looked at it and can remember what he did?"

As he dropped the spluttering vesta, he said, "Yes. It was not easy for Houdini because he was one man alone. Fortunately he was extremely strong. We are even more fortunate for there are two of us. The number and strength of the locks outside is academic, my dear Watson. What Houdini did was to notice that the doors were on pin hinges. In theory they could be lifted clear of the holding sites. To do this he extended the fingers of both his hands under the base of the locked doors. By exerting remarkable strength he was able to lift them clear, step outside and replace them! I am a strong man and so are you. Between us I believe we can do it."

Although the iron doors were incredibly heavy, we were able to extend our four sets of fingers through the space at the base and, on a signal from Holmes, we lifted them clear of their sockets. As we dropped those doors, so willingly, a rush of heavenly fresh air reached us but there was no time for rejoicing and we had to get clear before the gunmen returned. Holmes asked me if I had ever driven a motor van. I replied truthfully to the effect that I had driven a motor car. Holmes pushed me into the driving cab so that I sat behind the wheel. He climbed up into the single passenger seat and said, "It's up to you now old chap, get us out of here!"

I reversed, crashing out through the

flimsy garage gates and turned to take us away from that place at a steady twenty miles an hour. I had to slow down to negotiate a corner for we had reached the point where the gloomy street turned, to lead into one of similar darkness. As I slowed, Zoltan and his henchman leapt lightly onto the right-hand footboard. Zoltan leant through the opened window and brandished his revolver, saying, "I don't know how you did that but it has done you no good. I'm going to have to dispose of you now!"

There was an explosion, followed by another and Zoltan and his friend fell into the road. It was they, not we, who had been shot. I braked, although the van had been but crawling and we both leapt out to be greeted by a gunman; the very one who had dispatched Zoltan and his companion. My instincts as a medical man made me start back to see if there was any sign of life in the two fallen men but the newly arrived gunman brandished his weapon and signalled for us to follow. As we walked with him we made attempts at communication in English, German and French. He evidently understood only Hungarian and shouted at us in that language. "Out of the frying pan eh?" I muttered to Holmes.

"But while there is life eh, old fellow?" He was ever the optimist. The gunman walked us to a large saloon motor car, the make of which I cannot say. He pushed us into the back seats and drove with his left hand only on the wheel, the right holding his revolver pointed in our direction over his left shoulder.

Holmes muttered. "So you failed to bring your service revolver this time Watson?" I had to admit that I had surrendered it to the authorities some years before.

The big powerful car picked up speed as we drove through the outskirts of the city. Then suburbs gave way to open country where eventually there were occasional farms and vast fields of corn. After we had been driving for perhaps two hours (I did not dare make the movement required to take out and consult my watch), the country became even more open and almost wild. The few people that we passed appeared to greet the driver with a strange cross-armed salute which his driving and threatening activities prevented him from acknowledging.

The wild country gave way, ultimately, to a forest and we drove for many miles along a narrow track. Eventually the car stopped and we were ordered out. Our captor pushed us before him along a track, too narrow for the car, culminating in a footpath. Finally, we had not even this path to follow as he dragged us through a thicket. It was at this point that I turned suddenly and foolishly attempted to disarm him. Holmes was at my shoulder, backing me up, but the revolver eluded my grasp, was fired and unfortunately Holmes was wounded. As the gunman quickly regained his control of us I was happy to perceive — as I was just about able to in the semi-darkness — that Holmes had received only a glancing wound on his left forearm. He breathed, "Easy does it, my dear Watson, easy does it!"

Then, as we walked clear of the thicket, we suddenly saw that which it had concealed. It was a castle of most attractive and ancient appearance. We were marched across a moat by means of a drawbridge, which was raised as we entered the castle itself.

Inside we found ourselves in a huge hall, heated by a roaring log fire, around which sat persons of both sexes. I do not suggest that they were dressed in a style of a previous century but their clothing was far from modern with Magyar-style military uniforms much in favour. Our captor introduced himself and we quickly discovered that his refusal to converse in English had been deliberate and not because he did not understand that language.

"I am Captain Maroc, I have no idea who you are but I realized that you were enemies of the Magyar Straum and therefore entitled to rescue and interrogation. Who knows, I might have to shoot you myself, but at least you will get a fair hearing. Meanwhile, a comfortable room awaits you and in the morning we will decide what to do with you. What are your names?"

"My name is Sherlock Holmes and this is my friend and colleague, Doctor Watson." There was an uncomfortable silence followed by angry mutterings from the company present. It was evident that Holmes's exploits had reached this remote Magyar province but it was also evident that Holmes's introduction of ourselves was not accepted for its truth. Maroc said, angrily, "You will get nowhere here by exercising your British sarcasm. Now come with me to your room. I had decided to house you well but now I have changed my mind!"

Maroc all but pushed us down a

flight of rude stone steps and took us into what I can only describe as a dungeon from the Middle Ages. He swung shut and locked a huge wooden door to contain us. A minute or so later he returned with a candle, half a loaf of bread and a flask of water. He left these with us and I was glad that I was neither hungry nor yet thirsty.

Holmes grinned ruefully, his sharp features thrown into relief by the candlelight. "I say, Watson, rather exciting this last adventure of ours which may prove to be just that though I rather doubt it. I went to the cinema in Eastbourne a few months ago. The film was excellent, *The Prisoner of Zenda*. This apartment reminds me of a scene from the film, though I don't feel a bit like Lewis Stone. On the other hand, you have that pawky look, displayed by Rupert of Hentzau."

Despite my disgust at the light way in which he treated our predicament, I took the trouble to attend to his wound as best I could. I cleaned it with my linen handkerchief and some of the water from the flask. Then I tore some strips from that same article to bandage his forearm.

"Where are your Houdini secrets now, Holmes? Will they help us out of this scrape?" He lay down upon a pile of straw and actually started to go to sleep. I noticed a horrific great rat running across the floor; it must have weighed about two-and-a-half pounds. I pointed it out to Holmes, who opened one eye and said, "Ah yes, the common brown rat, *rattus vulgaris*." And with that he actually went to sleep.

A shaft of sunlight extending itself through a slit in an outside wall — a slit through which arrows would have been released — told me that it was day. I had not slept but had sat up all night by the light of the candle watching the rat and his many friends and relatives making regular excursions. They ate most of the bread that we had been left and I made no move to stop them. Holmes slept soundly and the rats gave him a wide berth, though I had no faith that they would do the same for me should I too lie on the straw.

Suddenly there were footsteps and the door swung open to reveal our old friends, Maroc and his revolver. He snapped a command, "Wake up, come with me!" We followed him obediently enough and he led us through the hall which we had seen the night before and into a further room: more splendid, beautifully furnished with huge antique chairs and silken embroidered wall hangings. Two extremely attractive women sat in chairs and serving people came and went. At the far end of the room stood a stocky figure in a military uniform who might have graced a comic opera. His back was to us, for he was gazing out of a window, the first in the castle that I had seen.

Maroc spoke, in reverent tones, "Your Highness, here are the two prisoners I told you about." Then he turned to us and said, "This is Prince Ehrich."

To my surprise, Holmes said, "Why yes, I had expected to see His Highness. How are you . . . Mr Harry Houdini?" The stocky figure turned and stood there, then leant forward from his waist, raising his head and bestowing upon us a most beatific smile, of the kind that had captivated several generations of theatre-goers. As for me, I fainted clean away for only the second time in my life (the first occasion being when Holmes reappeared before me, four years after plunging to his death over the Reichenbach Falls).

When I came to myself again, Holmes and Houdini were both leaning over me with some concern. Houdini almost carried me to a large, comfortable chair. He clapped his hands and ordered food and drink for us and soon the three of us were seated around a small table partaking of hot coffee, rolls and honey.

Houdini spoke first. "You had worked

it all out, eh Holmes, but you didn't let your pal in on it?"

I glared round at Holmes but he was at his most charming. "My dear old chap, my dear Watson, I know how you love to let all the facts trickle through to make a sudden stream of enlightenment. I wanted you to work it out for yourself. You would have too, given more time."

"But how could you guess?" I asked.

He was the old Holmes again now and all but snapped, "I never guess, I deduce and all my deductions led me to believe that Houdini was still alive. I realized that Zoltan had reached the point where he was bound to succeed in his attempts upon Houdini's life. The doctor from Hungary and his team were a rescue gang. Houdini, having agreed to the plan, was injected with a serum producing a cataleptic state. This even deceived his wife, Beatrice, and his body was whisked away and taken by train to New York. The story about the disfigurement was obviously untrue and, doubtless, Beatrice's own admission that she was somewhat intoxicated through most of the time, would explain the fact that she did not question the burial. Another injection even allowed a perfunctory medical survey and Houdini was buried in the special coffin with which he had been rehearsing. An hour or two after the mourners had departed the body, so called, was retrieved and Houdini was parachuted to a spot near this castle from his own private aeroplane."

I took all this in as if in a dream, trying to tell myself that truth is often stranger than fiction. Eventually I could stand no more and all but shouted, "Why, though, for God's sake? Why did this secret society wish to destroy Houdini and another organization wish to revere him and set him up in this castle?"

Houdini glanced enquiringly at Holmes. "You wish to answer or shall I?"

Holmes raised a hand. "I will

complete my narrative, then you can complete the story. I very quickly realized that there was some doubt concerning the Houdini birth date and country indeed of birth. The enquiry at the Budapest registry merely confirmed what I knew. As for this royal connection, the notes by Hardeen for a possible biography gave me the clue. Why did Samuel Weiss fight a duel with Prince Ehrich and his wife name a child Ehrich Prach (Ehrich Prince) just a few months later? I deduced that Houdini was really the son of Prince Ehrich, slain by his father. Something of this was known and many years later Houdini took his mother to Budapest and tried to introduce her to Magyar society. This was before the Great War, which changed Hungary from a monarchy to the attempted democracy that it is today. I realized that the secret society Magyar Straum wanted to destroy the only remaining heir to the throne, however vague that right of accession might be. But the royalists had their stronghold, in which we are at this moment."

I was still full of outraged suspicion. "You knew all this before we got to Hungary?"

Holmes smiled kindly. "Suspected but had to be sure. Do you remember that row of royal portraits at the embassy, which had somehow escaped being discarded by the new regime? The final portrait was of Prince Ehrich. The broad brow and piercing eyes convinced me that my suspicions were almost certainly justified. If I have missed any minor details I feel sure you can fill these in Mr Houdini, or should I say, Your Royal Highness?"

Houdini told his story, which agreed in practically all details with Holmes's narrative. He added, "When the medical team from the patriots arrived and explained to me that death by assassination would be inevitable if I did not fall in with their plan, it was not this fact alone that swayed me to go along with them. Mr Holmes, Doctor Watson, I was all but broke . . . yes, I the great Houdini! I had lost a fortune from producing my own movies, not just my own money but that of others. Further, in my fifties I no longer had the physical strength and energy to go back to doing all those sensational escapes and accepting all those challenges. I had reached the stage — and the age — when I could no longer stand upon a stage and proclaim, I am the Great Houdini, I challenge any public body or private individual to restrain me in such a manner that I am unable to free myself. I had slipped back into padding out my programme with magic tricks and illusions which are really old hat. The campaign against spook frauds created quite a bit of interest but I could tell that even this was losing its appeal gradually. Vaudeville houses were being converted into movie theatres and I had heard that some guy in Hollywood was producing a talking picture. I felt old, tired and could visualize a gradual return to the small time carnivals and circus even. This plan of theirs then presented me with an escape, my greatest ever. Moreover, it meant that Bess would end up rich, with all those policies that we had kept up. She may not have realized it but I was worth more to her dead than alive."

I could not help but interrupt and I suppose I may have been somewhat impolite when I said, "But look here my good chap, a fellow can't just leave his wife to grieve, thinking him dead whilst he is in fact not only alive but thriving (I gestured around me, to indicate the richness of our surroundings). The shock could have killed her, sir, and I regard you as a bit of a bounder!" I realized that I had overstepped the mark rather in being so critical of the actions of another, whose affairs were scarcely my business.

Houdini did not, however, take offence. "Doctor, I understand how it must seem to a gentleman like yourself. But please remember that I am not a gentleman born. I knew Bess was still fond of me in her way but I also knew that she was tired of travelling and could imagine her reaction if we had to go back to the stick and canvas life of earlier times. Oh, sure she is in delicate health you will say but that's her front, Doctor. If you were to test her heart, I'll wager you would predict that she will be around for another twenty years. She will miss me for a while but in the end she will be happier — and wealthy — at that."

"But do you not miss your wife, Mr Houdini?" asked Holmes.

The magician in prince's clothing replied, "Yes, but I have female company and I am expected to produce an heir. Now that is something that Bess was never able to help me with. There never was a little Houdini and there never will be but there might be a little Prince Ehrich."

Still somewhat shocked I said, "You do realize that we will have to return to America and inform Mrs Houdini of that which Holmes has discovered?"

"I suppose that bit could not be left out?" said Houdini, frowning.

"I am afraid not. You see I was engaged to investigate the possibility that your death had been caused deliberately, either directly or indirectly. Your wife has an insurance policy which will pay her half-a-million dollars if I can prove something of this kind."

Houdini started, then smiled hugely. "Good old Bess, I didn't know anything about such a policy but then she always was the shrewd one! Is it possible for you to go back to her and present it as fact that the Magyar Straum were responsible for my death? After all, it is a near truth, they tried very hard."

"The ethics of my profession," Holmes replied, "demand that I report back to my client everything that I have discovered. They do not, I feel, make it necessary for me to tell anyone else. The only crime that has been committed was by Maroc, in the shooting of Zoltan and his ally but as they were criminals and, in

254

any case, concern only an extremely suspect Hungarian regime I hardly feel obliged to tell anyone of that. However, I must warn you Mr Houdini that if, at any point, I am questioned by agencies of Great Britain or the United States I will be forced to answer their questions. Also I cannot assist your wife in claiming on that insurance policy, knowing such an action to be wrong."

Houdini grinned ruefully. "Well, I guess she has enough already but if she feels hard done by she can come here and share what I have, which is pretty good."

I could not help but say, "I wonder what she would think about your concubine and what would be her reaction to the birth of a future monarch?"

The subject was dropped for a while as Houdini showed us his kingdom and introduced us to some of his supporters. Maroc we had already met and he was full of apologies concerning our imprisonment in the rat-infested dungeon.

"I'm sorry but I thought you were here to expose His Highness, and I did not know then that you were to be trusted."

We saw the lake with its superb collection of waterfowl, the stables and carriages which were kept in perfect order for the coronation which Houdini's supporters evidently genuinely believed possible. The armoury contained no longer the collection of pikes and lances from the Middle Ages which it had been built to house; but rather a vast number of rifles, machine guns and boxes of ammunition and grenades. Maroc, who appeared to be the commander in chief of the small army said, "The dawn of freedom will come and when we are ready we will strike at the very heart of Budapest and capture the seat of government. Hungary will rise to support us that we may protect this great country from the rising tide of fascism which is beginning to threaten this continent. Already one such brigand has taken over the control of Italy. The great Austro-Hungarian Empire must be restored if it is to face up to these things. But the first stage will be the rebirth of Magyar royalty."

Despite the eight hundred years that had passed since its original construction, the Magyar castle's interior had been considerably modernized. The room to which we were shown was magnificent, with a private bathroom of which we had soon taken full advantage. Soap, towels and razors had been provided and the wardrobe contained suitable clothing for two gentleman tourists.

As Holmes removed his thirty-six-hour growth of beard he said to me, "Watson, I must apologize for keeping you in the dark but I really did think you would gain pleasure from your eventual realization of what had happened. When I first suspected the truth I almost wanted my findings to be a mistake. Of course I cannot wish that the very much alive Houdini had died as believed. But it would have made our next steps rather easier ones."

I said little. I had not completely forgiven Holmes for failing to keep me abreast of his discoveries, so I changed the subject, "I hope our luggage is safe at the City Centre Hotel." There was an answering, uninterested grunt from Holmes.

Later we partook of a magnificent meal in company with Houdini and the lady he introduced us to as the 'contessa'. She was, to use a rather lewd term, his mistress. She was a charming and extremely attractive woman, a refugee of noble blood from Romania. Houdini said, "My family were all but refugees when they arrived in the United States so I know how it feels to be looked upon as different by the rest of the population. Well, Contessa Irena and I have a lot in common and we now dwell here in peace, looked up to by all with whom we come into contact."

The wild grouse and artichokes would have passed as excellent if they had been served to us at Simpsons and the rather chianti-like wine of the district was superb. Houdini drank only the natural juices of lemons and limes. The opulence of his new environment had not changed his temperate tastes. Contessa Irene asked us many questions about our lives and experiences in Britain and America. She was particularly anxious to learn all she could about the women's fashions from the outside world. I could not help her much, being somewhat unobservant of such things but Holmes surprised me by giving her a really detailed idea of the current female styles of both dress and grooming.

I must have looked surprised, because he turned to me and said, "Well, after all, Watson, I am a detective. It is, or was, part of my business to notice everything around me. For example, I notice that Mr Houdini has not entirely forsaken his theatrical activities. He still gives at least an occasional performance, observing the full professional requirements."

Houdini's eyes narrowed. "Has Maroc or one of the others told you of my weekly performances? I just do a little magic to amuse my supporters. I have had a little theatre built in the courtyard."

"As I suspected and no, neither Maroc nor any other person has told me of this, I simply deduced it from observation. Watson knows my methods and will I feel sure explain." I must have blushed as I said, "Well, I will do my best. Mr Houdini is still in excellent physical shape for a man of his years, so he obviously has continued with those muscular diversions which have made him famous."

Holmes nodded. "Excellent Watson but I'll wager there is also a gymnasium in this splendid castle, or that which is used for the same purpose?"

"Please Mr Holmes, tell us how you

know that I still perform?" Houdini asked, grinning.

Holmes, himself a frustrated actor, waited until he felt that he had everyone's attention. Then he said, "If there is one thing in this world that gives away the trade of a professional theatrical it is his shirt. However much it is washed it will for a long time bear the traces of the five-and-nine greasepaints most often used. The collar shows this the most. Mr Houdini is wearing a shirt beneath his tunic which has been unbuttoned at the neck and I have observed the collar. Do you see those traces of pink cosmetic Watson?"

"Yes, but how do you know that the shirt is not one that Houdini used when he was still in the show business? You have said yourself that many washes often fail to remove the stains!"

"A good point, Watson, but just look at that shirt, perhaps you would open your tunic wider, Mr Houdini, that Watson might observe?"

Houdini was kind enough to remove the tunic and hang it upon the back of his chair. I saw that the shirt was not only of a rather unusual design, concerning its collar shape but also bore an embroidered Magyar crest where the breast pocket might have been.

After the meal Houdini took us into his portrait gallery where the rows of ancient paintings of long past royalty gave way to those only slightly faded, including one of Prince Ehrich, dated by the artist, 1868. Next to it hung a splendid newly painted portrait of Houdini in his comic opera uniform. It was dated 1927. The likeness between the two subjects of the portraits as they hung side by side was startling. Then as we reached the end of the long narrow gallery Houdini pointed dramatically at the end wall which was dominated by a huge contemporary portrait of a stately and elderly lady in a black ball gown, holding a black lace fan. Despite lines of trouble around her eyes her appearance was striking. A metal engraved plate below the picture proclaimed that it was of Queen Cecelia at the state ball in Budapest.

Houdini stood before the picture in reverence and said, "My sainted mother, just as she was so long ago when she was queen for a night. I had it painted from a photograph that I had taken of her, wearing Queen Victoria's gown."

That night we were taken to the theatre; a splendid bijou concert hall in the courtyard. There was an orchestra to play the overture and the fanfare which greeted Houdini's first entrance. He was dressed in a splendid tuxedo suit which, like all of his clothes, looked as if he had rolled around on the stable floor whilst wearing it. He turned upon the two-dozen-strong audience including ourselves that wonderful theatrical smile of his. To accompanying waltz music he produced a seemingly endless number of playing cards from thin air, culminating with a fan of a dozen cards. He conjured a number of ducks from an extremely innocent-looking foulard and materialized a great many large silk flags of all nations finishing with an even bigger one featuring a Magyar emblem. This produced much applause, as did the production of Contessa Irena from beneath it. The royal couple stood posed together as a number of doves were released from the back of the auditorium, flying onto the stage.

The contessa, following hypnotic passes from Houdini, was made to float in mid-air. She lay there, as if on an invisible couch, until Houdini clapped his hands causing her to vanish completely from our gaze. I was amazed, for it was so far in advance of anything I had seen at Maskelynes, where I had seen a similar illusion in which the floating lady vanished but only after she had been completely draped in a sheet.

In the second half of the programme, Houdini performed some of his escapes from handcuffs and leg irons, straight jackets and similar restraints. He and the contessa performed the Metamorphosis illusion made famous by Houdini and Bess in his early days. But this time an all glass trunk was used, the changeover of the performer and the assistant in the trunk was performed unbelievably quickly, with only a silk sheet passed before them instead of the use of a heavy draped cabinet.

The show went on and it became obvious to me that Houdini had developed a series of tricks and illusions which were streets ahead of those presented by contemporary conjurers, his own previous programmes included. Afterwards we congratulated him and he said with, for him, quite a degree of modesty, "I have a lot of time on my hands, plus the services of many brilliant craftsmen. With time and price no object, I can develop the most amazing conceptions. I'd love Howard Thurston or Harry Blackstone to see my new show, it would knock them out."

Much as we were enjoying our stay at Houdini's kingdom, we decided to leave on the following morning in order not to create unnecessary suspicion from the government's secret agents who would still, we imagined, be watching our hotel.

Houdini's parting words to us were, "So, be careful to tell only Bess that I am alive, for her own sake. Tell her she is welcome to come and live here if anything goes wrong with the other life policies, or for any other reason. You can mention that the barman mixes an excellent Martini, so I am told but if she refuses to believe you, as well she might, you can tell her that I told you the ultimate secret word that we arranged for me to say if I died before she did and got a chance to send a spirit message. Nobody, believe me Mr Sherlock Holmes, nobody knows what that word is, save Bess and myself." He moved Holmes aside from the company, myself included and evidently breathed the word into

Holmes' ear. When they returned he said, "She will scream for fifteen minutes when you first tell her that I am alive. From grief or gladness — who knows — but that is her normal reaction to anything stressful."

Our return to Budapest was by a rather more roundabout route than had been taken on our arrival which had, after all, not been planned. Just outside the forest, which hid the castle, we were transferred from the car to a horse-drawn vehicle which took us to the outskirts of Budapest. There we were left and advised to get a taxi. After perhaps half an hour we were able to engage an aged prewar taxi with an extremely elderly driver.

We arrived then by cab at the hotel, wearing the clothes that we had left it in (they had been laundered for us as the splendid borrowed garments might have raised some eyebrows). The clerk at the reception desk waved a hand to attract our immediate attention. He spoke in German, which he knew that

Holmes understood. "Herr Holmes, your bedroom was broken open and we had to send for the police. They searched the room, took your baggage and that of your friend. If you want to regain these things you must go to the police station, it is just around the corner . . . "

It was with some uncertainty that we entered the broken-down-looking police headquarters for that section of the city. I soon realized that we had been right in our uncertainty. The bombastic police sergeant behind the desk signalled to two constables to restrain us just as soon as we had announced our business. "So, Englishmen, explain just who you are and what your business is in the new Hungary and where are your travel papers?"

We placed our passports upon the desk but whilst he perused them it was obvious, and possibly fortunate, that our names meant little to him. He signed to the constables and said, evidently, in Hungarian, "Search them." The first thing he found in our pockets was Holmes's notebook. He flipped the pages and his eyes widened as he saw the drawing of the cross of the Magyar Straum. He returned the notebook and signalled his constables to release our arms. Then he returned our passports with dignity and saluted.

As we walked back to the hotel I said, "Lucky it turned out that way? I was afraid that the drawing of the cross might have an entirely opposite effect."

"It is, as we have heard, a right-wing reactionary group, possibly they have either frightened the police sergeant, or have him as an ally. It's as well that he found no clue to the Magyar royalists, for the government hates them as much as do the Magyar Straum! I believe, Watson, it would be as well for us to leave for Paris on the night train."

I had not seen Paris for a number of years and found that the aftermath of the most terrible conflict in history had left its mark. The artists still exhibited their work for sale near the Madeleine but the presence of so many visiting Americans had given the scene a commercial aspect. One could no longer tell the genuine starving artist offering his work from the consummate actor playing the part and offering swiftly completed and oft-repeated subjects. Indeed I had all but agreed to purchase a genuine Lautrec from a charming young lady who seemed not to realize its value when Holmes intervened and pointed out the modernity of the paint involved, saying, "If you tilt the painting so Watson, you will notice a certain sheen which oil paint when fully dried out does not present. The process takes at least a year and this painting is not quite that old, despite probable efforts towards artificial drying out."

It was fortunate that the lady appeared not to understand English too well but she could see that Holmes had lost her a sale and glared at him.

I managed to get Holmes to sit for a lightning artist who had sketches of Ernest Hemingway and Oscar Wilde pinned to his display board. He produced a splendid profile of my old friend to rival anything that had been produced by Paget or Elcock. The artist noticed the likeness but obviously thought it coincidental. Likewise, the photographer who offered his sitters a range of fancy dress. For a few francs he would garb one as Napoleon or Tom Mix. He rummaged in his trunk and produced a deerstalker and an Inverness cape. These he insisted upon draping over my friend. He even produced a vast Meerschaum to complete the picture. A crowd collected, none of them dreaming that they were looking at Sherlock Holmes in person but sure that here was the most amazing example of a doppelgänger that they had ever seen. A matron from Boston insisted on throwing an arm around my friend, saying, "Quick, take the picture, the ladies guild will sure be fooled into thinking that I was in Baker Square!" She thrust some francs at the delighted photographer who soon had a line of people waiting to be photographed with Sherlock Holmes's double. Holmes declined to take a share of the takings and also found himself forced to refuse a lucrative offer concerning his future.

A little later as we sat over *citron pressé* at a café table we discussed the incident of the photographer. I remarked to Holmes on his good fortune that public recognition seemed rare, save when he made a caricature of himself. He nodded. "I believe you have seen me attired in a deerstalker and Inverness perhaps three times in all the years of our association? We have Paget and the actor Gillette to thank for this image of me in the mind of the public. Without such props I can go where I please, untroubled by the notoriety which they present."

We travelled to New York on the French liner *Burgundy* in record time, the captain being determined to win some sort of blue ribbon. We attended only one social function, the fancy dress evening, as Sherlock Holmes and Doctor Watson. This time I wore the deerstalker and cape, whilst Holmes wore my bowler and sported a false moustache. Although we were much ridiculed, the situation appealed to Holmes's rather bizarre sense of humour.

Part Four

The Final Seance

BACK in New York we discovered that Beatrice Houdini was out of town, spending some time in Atlantic City with Sir Arthur and Lady Conan Doyle. Holmes was in no hurry to impart to her the news that could of course be for her ears alone. We passed the time pleasantly enough in what must be one of the most fascinating cities in the world. But not for Sherlock Holmes the tourist sights that alone I might have been tempted to sample. Instead we went to a violin recital and, heavily disguised, to a meeting of The Manhattan Deerstalkers. This proved to be a sort of appreciation society, devoted to the study and reinterpretation of the *Strand Magazine* episodes with which I had been concerned. The members — doctors, lawyers, businessmen and women — were an earnest crowd who appeared to read more into the episodes than had ever been intended. I had co-operated with Conan Doyle to produce these episodes for the entertainment and pleasure of thoughtful readers and had never expected to hear read such learned and investigative papers. One retired American army major put forward a theory that Doctor John Watson was in fact a woman, Jean Watson and an elderly cleric from New Jersey insisted that Holmes had actually been killed in the accident at the Reichenbach Falls, just as at first believed. "The Holmes you have heard of since then is an impostor!" he expostulated.

The final event of the evening, following a break for Hudson pies and cups of Baker Street Beverage, was a lecture by an elderly woman who doubtless believed that which she proclaimed.

"Friends and fellow Deerstalkers, I want to tell you all about my visit to

Great Britain and my quest to meet dear Mr Holmes and his partner the Doc. Elmer and I got to Baker Street on the first foggy morning of our visit. All around us there were people talking just like John Barrymore in *Hamlet*, except for some who I heard were called Orkneys and I guess they were from Scotland. They spoke quite differently from the others, dropping their aitches and tapping their noses with their index fingers in a most amusing manner. I asked one of these where I could find the home of Mr Sherlock Holmes. He said, 'Blimee Missus, doncha know he went hoff ter keep bees in Sussex?'

"'Since when?'" I asked.

"Then he suddenly became quite rude and shouted, 'Donkey's ears.' Which I took to be some sort of reference to Elmer's lobes! But the cop put us right, he was all done up in a Keystone Cop outfit and he consulted with some guy in golfing knickers and they agreed that dear Mr Holmes had indeed left town some years ago. When I asked if they could point out where he had lived they both pointed in different directions. Obviously Mr Holmes had instructed them not to divulge his old address to anyone. As there is no such place as 221b Baker Street I figure that it was just part of a bum steer from the medico!"

* * *

We stole away into the night, Holmes chuckling considerably, saying to me, "Oh Watson what have you done? That woman was just on the point of saying that she was sure that she spotted Moriarty on the underground railway!"

On the following day Beatrice Houdini returned from Atlantic City with the Doyles in tow. All three were full of excitement regarding a certain reverend gentleman with whom they had enjoined in several seances whilst at the resort. Bess (a name I cannot resist using in this narrative yet would never have used in direct address to that lady despite invitations to do so) said to Holmes, "This guy, the Reverend Bridger, is either genuine or the most talented hustler ever! I'm still sceptical. He claimed to get a message from Harry's mother, with a secret word that they had arranged between them. The word was 'forgive' and, as far as I know, nobody save Harry, Cecelia and myself ever knew about this. Harry would never, never, have divulged it to anyone and I don't think I ever did!"

Holmes frowned. "You say you do not think you did. Can you not be sure on this point?"

She glanced round, assuring herself that the Doyles were out of earshot. "Well, you know me, sometimes after two or three Martinis I tend to let things slip. But as I say, I don't think I ever spoke the word to anyone. By the way, how are you getting on with the investigation, any news for me yet Mr Holmes?"

Holmes spoke quietly, as if also wishing his words to be between the three of us only. "Dear lady, I am near to the point where I will give you a definite answer but I need another day or so."

At this point the Doyles interrupted by moving over to be completely within earshot of the quietest of converse. They were full of excitement regarding the seances with Bridger that they had attended. Sir Arthur said, "Watson, Holmes, I am arranging for another seance to take place tomorrow night at the Algonquin Hotel. You are both invited and I know that however sceptical you may be you will save your findings until the seance is over. There will be just my wife and I, yourselves and dear Mrs Houdini. Already Bridger has brought us in touch with the departed spirit of Houdini's mother, this time in no uncertain way as even you would have agreed had you been there. Tomorrow Bridger has promised to do his level best to attract that most elusive of all spirits, Harry Houdini himself!"

"We will of course attend and whatever our thoughts or findings we will keep them to ourselves, be assured Sir Arthur," promised Holmes.

During the short walk back to the Hotel Brownstone I asked my friend, "Holmes, why have you not told Mrs Houdini about our findings so that we can have done with this affair. Surely there could have been a right moment of privacy arranged?"

"Easily Watson, but I rather wish to attend the seance with the Reverend Bridger, which I feel sure we will find interesting. I do not believe that the good Beatrice will be happy with our news and would rather delay it until immediately before our departure. She is a woman of fiery temper at times I'll be bound and I am too old to endure the remonstrations."

Holmes showed every sign of being as good as his word regarding our impending swift departure when on the following morning he booked our tickets back to Southampton at the steamship office. When we got back to the Brownstone there was a message from Bess, demanding to see us.

Holmes slipped the desk clerk a dollar. "Should Mrs Houdini present herself in person, please inform her that we did not return here from our walk."

The clerk winked hugely. "Dame trouble, eh? Rely on me sport!"

We spent most of the rest of the day at Central Park Zoo, to my annoyance, having already exhausted my interest during Holmes's absence. "Why here?"

As we sat on a bench beside a huge, elliptic sea-lion pond my friend replied, "Can you think of anywhere in New York where we are less likely to bump into Beatrice Houdini?"

Short of a nunnery I could not. So I made the best of it all, eventually beginning to share Holmes's interest in the animal kingdom to a certain extent. His knowledge on such a vast variety of subjects has never, through the years, ceased to amaze me. For example, we were in the lion house, where two, to me identical, full-maned African lions occupied identical adjoining cages. Holmes pointed to one of them, saying, "Newly arrived, unlike the other *felis leo*, who has been here for quite a long time." I failed to see how he could possibly know this and doubted in any case that we could verify it, until a keeper arrived with some pieces of meat on a four-wheeled barrow. The keeper pitched a piece of meat into each cage and both beasts threw themselves upon their ration. As the two beasts lay devouring horse-flesh, the keeper cocked a thumb at one of them and said, "Ain't been here long but he's settlin' down nicely!"

As he pushed his cart towards the leopard cages I could only say, "How could you possibly have known, Holmes?"

"Oh come Watson, you know my methods and have always been at least a good observer of that which is in front of my eyes."

I scanned the two cages for some clue in the form of a notice reading, 'Received 6 July 1927' or something of the kind but no such notice was there.

"What were the two beasts doing prior to the appearance of their dinner trolley?" Holmes asked.

"Why the one was pacing up and down, whilst the other was sitting quietly."

Sherlock Holmes applauded. "Observation excellent but translation of that observed found wanting. My dear Watson, why was the pacing lion indulging in that pastime?"

"Well, I assumed that he was doing it because he was in despair at being caged."

"Not so, Watson, in the wild a lion sleeps twenty hours a day and spends the other four hours hunting an antelope or zebra. The energetic lion is simply doing what his instinct tells him to, pacing for the four hours which precede the appearance of the dinner cart, which long domicile here has suggested as inevitable. This behaviour in a zoo keeps the animal in perfect condition. The other lion, now, has been recently captured and transported from his native Africa. He has already learned to enjoy the meat when it is presented to him but it will take a few days, nay even weeks more before he anticipates its time of arrival. Shortly, he too will begin an excited pacing to and fro of his cage for several hours." As ever the answer had been simple, yet had required more effort than anticipated.

We dined, if indeed the word can be applied to that which we consumed; though on reflection I think it can be due to the name of the establishment which we patronized. It was proclaimed to be Joe's Diner and proved to be a sort of refurbished railway carriage. We sat upon revolving stools at a counter, across which leant a large red-faced man with equally fiery hair and moustache.

"What would youse guys like . . . how about a couples of boigers?" he enquired jovially.

As he prepared what appeared to be rissoles inside a sort of unsweetened bun, I remarked to Holmes upon the singularity of his accent.

"Irish father, Greek mother, Watson: notice the S added to many words which is typical of the Greek immigrant," he replied.

"And the Irish?" I asked.

"The colour of his hair, his general appearance, plus the use of the expression 'youse' which is prevalent in Dublin."

"Could he not have an Irish mother and a Greek father?"

But Holmes thought this unlikely. "The Irish in him predominates." Holmes's smugness in these deductions, following so closely upon the episode with the lions, irked me. Was my friend becoming what the Americans call a smart alec?

I leant across and asked the man, "Excuse me sir, might I enquire your name?"

"Joe . . . Joe Casey . . . put it there pal!"

He extended a huge red hand, which I shook. As for Holmes, he sat upon his revolving stool with an expression of triumph upon his sharp old face.

Suitably bathed, shaved and formally attired we presented ourselves at the Algonquin at the appointed time. I was happy to be with Sir Arthur and his gracious lady again, even if a trifle uncomfortable in the thought that I might have some small part to play in their disillusionment. Honest, decent and crusading people, their genuine sincerity in their beliefs concerning spiritualism had never been in question. But there are sharks in this world of ours who cannot always be recognized as such even by shrewd and discerning minds. My long collaboration with Sir Arthur in the preparation of the adventures, exploits and experiences of my friend Sherlock Holmes had shown me how agile he was in detecting subtle deception, for example, in the revelations in the adventure of *The Red Headed League* and the seemingly supernatural events concerning that great ghostly *Hound of the Baskervilles*. He had appreciated these deceptions, their motives and the mechanics of them. Why, oh why did he appear to have such a blind spot when dealing with those who claimed to conjure up the spirits of the dear departed?

Beatrice Houdini introduced us to the Reverend Joshua Bridger. He was a personable young man, neatly attired in clerical dress, with a full head of beautifully groomed chestnut hair. His gold-rimmed pince-nez dangled from around his neck upon a silken cord, save when he raised them to peer through, rather like a duchess with a lorgnette. He spoke with a southern American accent, bordering on the benevolent.

Eventually, all niceties of etiquette

having been observed, we all repaired to the small room which had been prepared for the seance. There was a little table but none of the impedimenta of illusion so often provided by the professional medium. There were no cabinets, trumpets or indeed anything in the room save the table and a number of matching chairs. The single window was heavily draped with black material so that the room could be plunged into complete darkness at the touch of a switch. Before this happened, the Reverend Bridger made a speech:

"Dear friends, we are gathered here tonight, united in one purpose, that of contacting the spirit of our dear, departed brother, Harry Houdini. I am the only one among us who knew him not in his earthly life. Despite this I am confident that I will succeed in my efforts. If Houdini comes through for us it will be a great triumph, to eclipse even that which some of us recently experienced in Atlantic City, where I was able to coax the spirit of Houdini's dear mother, Cecelia, to not only converse with us but to speak a secret word known only to Mrs Houdini as far as the living are concerned. As you know, Houdini in life was full of doubt . . . doubt about the existence of spirits even, save alone their ability to contact the living. In truth, his doubts were so strong as to build a wall between himself and the spirit world. That is why he never found a medium in whom he could believe. You do not greet even a living friend by saying, 'I do not believe in you'! To infer as much to a delicate spirit would guarantee that no contact would be made. But there is no such impediment here tonight. After all those present, who are not perhaps convinced believers, have at least completely open minds. I feel this, I sense it and for this reason I am optimistic that we will be successful. In order to assure you all that there is no deception I would draw your attention to the fact that I use no intrinsic aids in my work. There are no rapping hands, planchettes, dark cabinets or slates and, to quote our dear departed himself, I have nothing up my sleeves."

He rolled up the sleeves of his jacket and gave us all an arch glance. This produced polite chuckles from Sir Arthur and myself and a sort of disguised choking sound from Bess.

The Reverend Bridger concluded by saying, "If I am able to contact Houdini he will be able to speak directly to us, although you may not recognize his voice as that with which he spoke when he took earthly form. This is quite often the case with spirits. Well now, let us begin to work. Mr Holmes, you are nearest to the light switch, would you be so kind as to plunge us into that friendly darkness which so much aids our concentration?"

As Holmes pushed up the switch I reviewed the situation in my mind. As Holmes and I alone among us knew Houdini to be still very much in the land of the living we of course had to completely discount any sort of spirit message from him. If no such message was received Bridger might prove to be a genuine and sincere person. But if any message transpired, purporting to be from Houdini, he had to be a fraud.

There was a silence, as complete as was possible in a large and busy New York hotel. No sound was heard for perhaps two minutes, save those of shifting feet and the rustling of the ladies' dresses. Then Bridger's voice was heard, with an even more dramatic timbre: "I call upon my spirit guide, Chief Eagle Hawk, to aid me in finding one spirit among millions, the one spirit among them that we hope and pray to contact. Are you there Chief Eagle Hawk, please speak to us!"

After some ten seconds or so a grunting monosyllabic voice was heard, "I am here brother Bridger, who is it you wish to contact?"

The reverend gentleman's all but natural voice resumed, "Chief, please bring to us the spirit of our dear brother Harry Houdini, bring him here through the space of eternity to speak to us. His dear wife Beatrice is here, as are his friends Sir Arthur and Lady Conan Doyle, yes and two more friends from Britain, Mr Sherlock Holmes and Doctor Watson. Please entreat dear Harry to speak to us."

The obliging Indian chief spoke again, "Brother Bridger, friends, I have Harry Houdini's spirit at my side. Please speak to him."

Again Bridger's all but natural voice implored, "Dear brother Harry, please speak, please say something to your dear wife who is here tonight."

What next occurred somewhat startled me I confess. For the voice which purported to be that of Houdini was as unlike his actual speaking voice as it might be possible for it to be. The tones were those more reminiscent of a Shakespearian actor than a vaudeville showman. It was a rich voice, rather like that of Sir Henry Irving yet with a transatlantic touch.

"Beatrice, dear Beatrice, I am here, your own Harry! I guess I may sound a little different sweetheart, to the way I did in life but that is the way it is here. However to assure you that I am here, let me remind you of the words of our secret code, the one we used in our thought transference act, long, long ago. The words were, Rosabelle, answer, tell, pray, answer, look, tell, answer, answer, tell! Am I right?"

Bess breathed, rather than said, "Yes."

The voice purporting to be that of Houdini continued, "Bess after I have returned to the spirit world, please remove your wedding ring and show our friends the word engraved on the inside of the band. The word is Rosabelle and you can tell the others what it means. You have never told anyone of this word, or yet shown anyone the inside of your ring! I want you to pay great attention to everything that dear brother Joshua Bridger tells you. He is a good man and can advise you as to certain matters concerning your future. I love you dear Bess, I must leave you for now but I will, God willing, be back to speak with you again . . . goodbye darling . . . sweet Rosabelle!"

The voice grew gradually less in volume and finally Bridger spoke, "Please put on the light Mr Holmes, I am so weary and must rest."

As Holmes switched on the light I observed that Bridger was sitting limply in his chair, presenting an appearance of complete exhaustion. "Dear sister Beatrice, please remove your wedding ring that we may confirm that which dear brother Harry has told us."

Bess removed her ring, without much difficulty and cast it onto the table with an almost dramatic gesture. Sir Arthur asked her permission to examine it and having been granted it, scrutinized it carefully. Then he passed it around, saying, "You will see that the word Rosabelle is indeed engraved upon the inside of the band."

Holmes peered at the inner side of the ring through his lens and agreed that the word was the correct one. "Mrs Houdini, could you perhaps confirm that nobody has ever seen the inside of the ring since it was engraved?"

She nodded. "The words that Harry spoke were the ten words of a two-person telepathy code that we used about thirty-five years ago. With these words and their variations and different combinations he could convey almost anything to me as I sat blindfolded upon the stage. For instance, "Rosabelle. Answer. What is this?" would be a watch. "Pray, tell," was a man and "Tell, pray," was a woman. Just a simple code, nothing fancy."

The Reverend Bridger began to recover his strength and we removed ourselves to the hotel lounge where Bess plied him with coffee. The Doyles were full of praise for Bridger, saying that they would look forward to further seances. I was curious about the name

Rosabelle and asked Bess, "What is the significance of this name that would cause Houdini to have it secretly engraved into a ring for you?" Bess was on her third Martini since the end of the seance. "It was to do with a song that my girl partner and I used to sing when we were the Rahner sisters. The first time Harry met me he heard us sing it." Somewhat to our general embarrassment, she started to sing in a grating soprano that attracted more than a little attention . . .

Rosabelle, my Rosabelle,
I love you more than I can tell,
Over me you cast a spell,
I love you, sweet Rosabelle.

Wisely the Doyles decided to call it a night, wagging fingers at Holmes concerning his lack of absolute faith in the wonders of spiritualism.

Sir Arthur said, as they departed in quest of a cab, "Holmes the only thing that has ever even threatened to mar our friendship has been your scepticism regarding the supernatural in general and spiritualism in particular. Now that you have had absolute proof I feel that we can become far closer. You know poor dear Harry always upset me greatly with his attitude towards mediums. Oh I grant you he exposed one or two obvious frauds but a couple of swallows do not make a summer and he had no right to make some of the accusations that he did, against really sincere and honest people."

Then he turned to Bridger. "My dear sir, can we give you a lift somewhere in our taxi cab?"

After this general exodus, Bess ordered more coffee for us and yet another Martini for herself. It was to me that she first spoke. "What do you make of all that Doc?"

"I find it all astounding!" I replied, in all sincerity.

I did. For had I not been conversing with a very much alive Harry Houdini but days earlier I would have been convinced that only his spirit could have made possible that which the seance had revealed. I asked Bess to tell us a little more about the code and the thought-reading act.

"Well Doc, I'll tell you. In the very early days, Harry and I were part of a circus troupe. Harry was the magician, did his escapes, was ringmaster and played the wild man in the sideshow. As for me I used to assist Harry but I also used to work with the clowns in a boy's Eton suit. We got about twenty bucks a week for the two of us, plus cakes, that's carny slang, means we got fed. Oh yes and in addition to the show we had to help put the tent up and pull it down. Even so it was OK until we stopped getting paid. Business fell off and the owner ran out of dough. Then one day he just upped and disappeared. The show was sold off by auction and Harry and I were stranded what seemed like a million miles from home. But Harry was a fighter and figured a way for us to get out of trouble. I was a pretty good mitt reader, you know, palmist and, for a while, we worked out of doors, in town squares in hick towns, me reading palms and Harry doing anything he could: magic, escapes and thought reading. That's how we started with the code. Soon we discovered that by playing on the superstitions of the country folk we could do better as spirit mediums!"

I was shocked. "You mean you held seances?"

"Sure, we'd hire a hall and advertise a seance and get a bigger crowd than we could have got for any other kind of show. We would start with the thought-reading routine, using the code with me convincingly blindfolded. Then we would pretend to get messages from the dear departed and we even got the names right by mooching around graveyards in the dark and reading the inscriptions with a flashlight. We'd find someone who had died fairly recently, find out all we could about them and dish the information up as a spirit message. Then we would make a collection, which was usually quite good (remember we let them in for nothing). Finally, the blow-off — that's carnival slang for the jam on the bread."

Holmes had been quiet but now he spoke. "What did you do, give private consultations?"

"I'll say we did and I always held back a few bits of local gossip about the departed just for this. I'd work in a dressing room. The people would come out and rave about how amazing it all was. We'd charge a dollar a time in some places. The women would eat out of my hand. The men, they weren't quite so easy but I'd let them get just a little bit familiar with me in the darkened room. Oh nothing serious, just enough for them to be on my side. Of course we were not proud of any of this but it might give you some idea as to why Harry was so knowledgeable about fake spiritualists, although over the years he had tried to forget the whole affair. I guess his campaign was some sort of exorcism. Unlike Harry, I go along with these people, I need the publicity if I'm ever going to get back into some sort of business. Many hundreds of people must have seen our thought-reading act. Some of them were magicians who would have recognized the code for what it was and could even remember all ten words and their order."

"My dear Mrs Houdini you have saved me the trouble of voicing my own thoughts concerning the code. But now we come to the matter of the ring and the engraving inside it. Did you ever speak to Bridger about this?"

"Sure, I told him about the word inside but I never told him what it was!"

"Quite so and was it in Atlantic City that you told him?"

"Sure!"

"But you have taken it off recently, perhaps for the first time in years?"

"How can you tell?"

"You slipped it off after the seance without much difficulty. Yet its scar upon your finger told me that it had remained there for many years undisturbed. I deduce therefore that it was recently removed, for the first time in many years."

"You are right, I was out shopping in Atlantic City with the reverend. He steered me into a jewellers, saying he wanted me to look at some tie pins and give him my thoughts on them as a present for his nephew. While we were there the storekeeper offered to clean the ring for me for free. It was a bit of a job for me to get it off but I don't pass up a free offer. He cleaned it and I slipped it back on but Sherlock, old sport, Bridger was still across the store from me, looking at the tie pins."

"Quite, he had previously bribed the storekeeper before steering you in there, to glimpse the word in the ring. Remember, you had already told Bridger that this secret word existed."

I thought that Bess took all this very

calmly, almost as if she did not care that she had been duped.

"He is an ingenious son of a gun isn't he? A man after my own heart."

"That might be only too true Mrs Houdini, a fortune hunter if ever I saw one."

This seemed to irk Bess a little. She finished her fourth Martini and said, "OK, Mr Holmes, let's have a little seance — you be the medium and show us what *you* can do in that direction."

To my utter amazement Holmes agreed to this. Of course I realized that he had been putting off the evil moment when he must tell Bess of our findings but I felt this was going a bit far.

Holmes went through a sort of pretence at going into a trance, then said, "I call upon the spirit of Harry Houdini to whisper to me a secret word, something that passed between his dear wife and himself, which nobody else could possibly know!" Then he relaxed and said, "Houdini whispered this secret word into my ear and Mrs Houdini, I am obliged to whisper it to you also."

Bess's expression was enigmatic; she leant her expensively coiffured head nearer to his. I saw his lips move but could not read anything from them, as a deaf person might have been able to. What happened next came as a great shock to me. Beatrice Houdini brought her right hand across Holmes's face with a resounding slap. His prominent cheekbone seemed to redden but he was as impassive as the wooden Indian that we had passed daily outside the cigar store. Her hand fell slowly to her lap, her face alert, her eyes huge and dilated. After what seemed like an age she spoke: "The sonofabitch is alive, ain't he?" Holmes nodded gravely.

I tried to calm the atmosphere by saying, "Dear lady, you must be delighted to know this?" She did not answer me but gave me a look that bordered upon hatred.

Between us Holmes and I told her of our discoveries in Hungary. Everything indeed that had happened during the week or so that had passed. She asked many questions which were answered by one or other or both of us with accuracy, yet still her wonder and, to some extent, her resentment grew. At length there was little more to tell her, save of Houdini's invitation for her to join him if she so wished.

She all but snorted, "He's gotta be kiddin'! Does he suppose I want to live in some draughty old castle and watch him and this Mazurka, or whatever her name is, produce kids? Oh no. I hired you to find me the proof that I wanted, proof that Harry had been rubbed out so that I could be a really wealthy woman. Well, so I have to settle for a little less than that, always assuming that you keep your mouths shut about Harry. How much is *that* going to cost me?"

I was shocked at her inference of possible blackmail but Holmes took it calmly. "Mrs Houdini, you asked, nay implored me to make certain investigations. I have made them and what I have found out has not been to your liking; indeed it would all have been better left alone. But unless I am directly questioned by some authority with the right to demand answers of me, my work is done. I cannot anticipate my part in any of this being of interest to police or government."

She was relieved, arose and began to walk somewhat unsteadily towards the lobby. Before gaining that objective she turned and said, "Mr Holmes, you will be getting my cheque. Oh and say, I'm sorry I belted you one!"

We stayed a little longer in the lounge of the Hotel Algonquin where Bess's bizarre outbursts had gone all but unnoticed beside those of its regular denizens, the Benchleys, the Hemingways and others of their kind. We discussed, Holmes and I, the whole incredible affair of the Houdini birthright. We drained the coffee pot and Holmes charged his pipe in anticipation of the short journey to the Hotel Brownstone.

"Holmes, now that this affair is concluded do you feel able to confide to me the secret word that Houdini imparted for Bess's ears alone?"

"Oh yes, as my oldest, nay only friend, I feel that I can trust you not to disclose it to anyone else, especially to the readers of your incredibly romanticized versions of my exploits!" He leant over and whispered a single word in my ear. He need hardly have worried, for I could hardly disclose it in print but let me just say here and now that I am hardly surprised that Beatrice Houdini clouted him.

THE END

A GENTEEL LITTLE MURDER
Philip Daniels

Gilbert had a long-cherished plan to murder his wife. When the polished Edward entered the scene Gilbert's attitude was suddenly changed.

DEATH AT THE WEDDING
Madelaine Duke

Dr. Norah North's search for a killer takes her from a wedding to a private hospital.

MURDER FIRST CLASS
Ron Ellis

Will Detective Chief Inspector Glass find the Post Office robbers before the Executioner gets to them?

A FOOT IN THE GRAVE
Bruce Marshall

About to be imprisoned and tortured in Buenos Aires, John Smith escapes, only to become involved in an aeroplane hijacking.

DEAD TROUBLE
Martin Carroll

Trespassing brought Jennifer Denning more than she bargained for. She was totally unprepared for the violence which was to lie in her path.

HOURS TO KILL
Ursula Curtiss

Margaret went to New Mexico to look after her sick sister's rented house and felt a sharp edge of fear when the absent landlady arrived.

THE DEATH OF ABBE DIDIER
Richard Grayson

Inspector Gautier of the Sûreté investigates three crimes which are strangely connected.

NIGHTMARE TIME
Hugh Pentecost

Have the missing major and his wife met with foul play somewhere in the Beaumont Hotel, or is their disappearance a carefully planned step in an act of treason?

BLOOD WILL OUT
Margaret Carr

Why was the manor house so oddly familiar to Elinor Howard? Who would have guessed that a Sunday School outing could lead to murder?

THE DRACULA MURDERS
Philip Daniels

The Horror Ball was interrupted by a spectral figure who warned the merrymakers they were tampering with the unknown.

THE LADIES
OF LAMBTON GREEN
Liza Shepherd

Why did murdered Robin Colquhoun's picture pose such a threat to the ladies of Lambton Green?

CARNABY
AND THE GAOLBREAKERS
Peter N. Walker

Detective Sergeant James Aloysius Carnaby-King is sent to prison as bait. When he joins in an escape he is thrown headfirst into a vicious murder hunt.